# STAGE RAIDER

The stage out of Harper's Town bound for Rainwater was late leaving — a bad omen for driver Charlie Deakin. The passenger list caused him further anxiety, including as it did the troublesome banker Willard Pierce and his provocative wife Madelaine; the salacious storekeeper, Lemuel Buthnott; the stranger, Holden; and gunslinger Mr Jones. Then there was the desert route, which Charlie hated, and the prospect of unwelcome riders approaching fast in a cloud of dust. Bad omens could sometimes only get darker . . .

*Books by Luther Chance*
*in the Linford Western Library:*

GUN RAGE
HUCKERMAN'S NOON
ROGUE COLT
OCACHI'S RUN
THE JACKSON RAID
TRAIL-SCARRED
THE GUN MASTER
BROKEN NOOSE

# LUTHER CHANCE

# STAGE RAIDER

*Complete and Unabridged*

LINFORD
*Leicester*

First published in Great Britain in 2006 by
Robert Hale Limited
London

First Linford Edition
published 2007
by arrangement with
Robert Hale Limited
London

British Library CIP Data

Chance, Luther
   Stage raider.—Large print ed.—
Linford western library
   1. Stagecoach robberies—Fiction
   2. Western stories 3. Large type books
   I. Title
   823.9′14 [F]

   ISBN 978–1–84617–852–8

Published by
F. A. Thorpe (Publishing)
Anstey, Leicestershire

Set by Words & Graphics Ltd.
Anstey, Leicestershire
Printed and bound in Great Britain by
T. J. International Ltd., Padstow, Cornwall

This book is printed on acid-free paper

*This one for T. M.*

# 1

Merv Hinks cleared his throat carefully, glanced over his spectacles at the clock on the wall and consulted his timepiece for the fifth time in as many minutes.

'Sorry about this, folks,' he smiled weakly, his gaze moving over the faces watching him, 'it ain't usual, I can assure you. Company's very particular about time-keepin'. Success of the line depends on it. Yessir.'

Merv glanced at the wall clock again, consulted his timepiece once more, twitched his shoulders and winced at the sudden stickiness of the shirt on his back.

A man wearing a tailored frockcoat, silk shirt, grey homburg and immaculately creased trousers over polished shoes and spats, slapped his knees with an air of finality and stood up.

Merv swallowed. He had been

expecting this; no, he had been dreading it. He had seen it coming way back, and now Willard King Pierce, first president of the State and County Bank founded right here in Harper's Town, was on his feet and looking decidedly menacing.

'Mr Hinks,' he began, his voice filling the stage office like a sudden clap of thunder, 'if time means so much to this line, then why, pray, are you taking it upon yourself to delay — without explanation thus far — the departure of the scheduled stage service between here and Rainwater, which is now, by my reckoning' — he flourished his own gold-plated time-piece from his waistcoat pocket — 'currently some twenty minutes late loading, let alone leaving? Is there an explanation? If not, why not? If so, what in the name of tarnation is it and may we please hear it?'

Pierce replaced his timepiece, settled his grip on the lapels of his coat, and glared.

Merv sweated. His shirt had plastered itself to his back, his legs were weak and threatening to buckle. He had a sudden desire to turn and run, but nothing like the strength to do it. He pushed his spectacles to the bridge of his nose and gazed at the faces still watching him.

Seated directly opposite was the young and strikingly beautiful wife of Willard Pierce, Madelaine, her expression unmoving save for the tantalizing half smile at her full and softly parted lips. Merv carefully averted his gaze from the ample cleavage she displayed in the flawless cut of her velvet dress.

To Mrs Pierce's left sat a small, neat fellow with a slightly ashen face, a rapidly expanding paunch, fidgety hands and furtive eyes. This was Lemuel Buthnott, proprietor of the Harper's Town mercantile, a softly spoken man who lived under the strict regime and domination of his wife, Agatha, and had done so for close on forty years. He continued to survive the matrimonial rigours, however, and was now on his annual visit to his suppliers in Rainwater. It was an escape and, on this occasion, a chance to enjoy Madelaine Pierce's cleavage at close quarters.

Alone in the shadowed corner of the office sat Frank Holden. He had shown up in town on the through stage to Winnecutt some four days back, booked in at the Harper's Hotel, drank alone, slept alone and generally kept himself to himself. He was tall, weathered, and might have been anything. Hard to say. He had certainly paid Madelaine Pierce no attention whatsoever, even though her gaze wandered his way more than once.

'Well, Mr Hinks,' boomed Pierce again, 'like the stage, we're all waiting.'

Merv adjusted his spectacles and gripped the sides of his narrow desk. 'T'ain't easy for me in my capacity as line clerk on these occasions,' he croaked, clearing his throat through the words. 'Not easy at all. There's considerations and understandin's and there has to be some measure of leeway; give and take. Hell — beggin' your pardon, Mrs Pierce — where would we be without some give and take?'

'Three miles down the trail to the station at Bloodrock right now if the stage had left on time!' clipped Pierce, to the amusement of Buthnott and Holden. Mrs Pierce took a fringed lace handkerchief from her clutch bag and dabbed delicately at her neck. She was aware of Buthnott's gathering stare.

Merv's spectacles slid from the bridge of his nose. 'Well, o'course, you're right, Mr Pierce, dead right. In fact, spot on.' He took his timepiece in a shaking hand. 'Three miles to the inch at this time by my reckonin'.' He paused, wilting under the stares of the passengers. 'Even so, you can bet your sweet life to Charlie Deakin and Moose Topper makin' up the time just as soon as they get that outfit out there movin'. Yessir, ain't a finer stage team in the business than Charlie Deakin and Moose Topper. Best driver, sharpest fella ridin' shotgun in the territory. Won't find better, not nowhere and they are your team for the entire journey! I'd sure as sun-up place a lot of store by that. You bet. Only the best, eh, Mr Pierce?'

The banker gritted his teeth. 'We are still waiting, Mr Hinks,' he growled. 'What is the cause of the delay?'

'Me,' came a voice from the open door. 'I'm the cause.'

# 2

He was dark.

He wore dark clothes, a black broad-brimmed hat, black boots. His face too was dark, swarthy, weathered and pitted as if at one time buried for an age in gravel. But it was the man's dark eyes and the stare that seemed to penetrate through shadow that held the attention of those gathered in the stage office at Harper's Town.

Merv Hinks was the first to break the silence. 'Ah, Mr — '

'Jones,' said the man without looking at Merv.

'Mr Jones. Yes, well that'll do fine, sir. If we can just take your luggage.'

'No luggage.' The man's stare had shifted to Madelaine Pierce and burned into her like flame.

'Travellin' light, eh?' smiled Merv. 'Well, that's the way some folk prefer it. Now — '

'Before you proceed, Mr Hinks,' bristled Willard Pierce, tightening his grip on the lapels of his coat, 'perhaps Mr Jones would care to explain why he has kept us waiting and delayed the departure of this stage by nearly three-quarters of an hour. I think we are deserving of at least that courtesy.'

Merv swallowed and sweated. Lemuel Buthnott fidgeted. Frank Holden simply watched. The man's stare cruised like a light to Pierce's face and settled without blinking.

'A hand of poker,' he said, and switched the stare back instantly to Madelaine Pierce.

'A game?' blustered Pierce, his hands sliding from his lapels to his sides. 'You delayed the stage and us for a game of poker?'

'Must've been some heavy stakes there,' said Holden.

'They were,' said the man. 'A fella's wife.'

There was a moment's silence in which the stage passengers and Merv could only stare wide-eyed, Buthnott with his mouth open, Madelaine Pierce with her cheeks flushing to a bright crimson.

'You mean to say a man staked his wife in a game of poker?' croaked Pierce.

'He did,' said the man.

'And did you win?' quipped Holden.

The man's stare did not move. 'I won,' he said. 'Gave her back. Didn't fancy her.'

Madelaine Pierce hid a soft smile discreetly behind her handkerchief. A jumble of words and indignation fumed in her husband's throat threatening to choke him. Buthnott fumbled in his pocket for a bandanna. Holden grinned.

Merv pushed back his spectacles and rustled paperwork. 'Yeah, well, time you folk were boardin'. Got to make it to Bloodrock by nightfall. And I guess Charlie's more than anxious to get the team movin'. So if you'll all step this way and just follow me. That's right,

9

folks, this way. And may I wish you all a safe and pleasant journey. You bet!'

★　★　★

Charlie Deakin had been involved with the stage for most of his working life, and done most things pertaining to keeping the teams healthy, fresh and renewed wherever and whenever necessary, the coaches themselves clean and greased, the tack gleaming. He had even worked a swing station for a time, and once in a dire emergency, taken over Merv's job as clerk in the line office.

Now Charlie was the company's senior driver and highly regarded as a man who knew more about the line, its functioning and well-being, not to mention the territory between Harper's Town and Rainwater, better than anyone. Charlie Deakin was the recognized authority.

But on this run, as the scheduled stage pulled out of town for its first stop

10

and overnight stay at Bloodrock, he was not a happy man.

For one thing, the stage was already running close on an hour late out of Harper's Town all thanks to that poker playing sonofabitch, Mr Jones. God-damn him! He was going to be trouble; he could smell it.

Second was the passenger list. Now, he had no way of controlling who did or did not travel with the line. They all paid his wages whoever they were. But, hell, he had sure as moonlight drawn the short straw when Willard King Pierce and his wife had signed up to make the three-day journey to Rainwater.

Of all the luck . . . It was one thing having Pierce himself on board with all his grumbling, fetish for time-keeping and endless reminders that no one should forget that he personally had helped bankroll the line in the first place. He was bad enough.

But then there was his wife.

No denying Madelaine Pierce was

one hell of a woman; just about as beautiful and alluring as any who had ever set foot in the territory, let alone Harper's Town. And half Pierce's age. Which is where the trouble had started.

It was a fact, plain as the nose on your face, that Madelaine Pierce found all men younger than her husband an attraction to be tempted and toyed with at her whim. Only man in town who seemed unaware of this was Willard himself. Or maybe he only seemed not to notice.

Consequence had been, and still applied, was that the men of Harper's Town were constantly vying for so much as a glance from those flashing blue eyes, and Madelaine Pierce dished them out like loose change. Men confined with her for three days in a stage at the height of the hot, sticky season spelled double trouble.

Of the others who had boarded late that afternoon, only Lemuel Buthnott was a face Charlie knew. Buthnott was a hen-pecked, dominated fool and was always glad to be making his yearly trip to Rainwater. He would sit tight, stay silent and fuss at the feet of Madelaine Pierce like a lap dog.

But what of Holden and Mr Jones?

Very little of one, nothing at all of the other. Holden had been resident at the hotel for a few days where Boots, the porter and odd job man around the place, had reported that the fellow had slept, eaten, drank quality whiskey, slept some more, taken a stroll round town, then booked his passage on the stage for Rainwater. If he had spoken half-a-dozen sentences during his stay, that had been the limit.

The man calling himself Mr Jones, on the other hand, was quite another pan of beans.

Jones had simply drifted into town from no one knew where. Could have been any place. He had the mark of a gambling man and some reckoned a gun for hire if the price was right from the outset. And proved it in a string of winning hands at the poker table, culminating in Eli Carney's stake of his wife in the last hand to be played. Jones, of course, had won, but refused to collect the stake on the grounds that a woman was a baggage he had no time for — much, it was said by some, to Dora Carney's disappointment. She had been desperate to be free of Eli for some long time.

And thus the still largely unknown Mr Jones had been the last to join the stage.

Charlie had made known his feelings to his long-time partner and shotgun rider, Moose Topper, long before the outfit had left Harper's Town and was still grumbling five miles down the trail as he reined the team through Candyman's Drift.

'Been drivin' this outfit Harper's Town to Rainwater more years than I care to recall and I ain't never, not never, been more than seven minutes late pullin' out. You hear that, Moose, *seven minutes*. And here we are an hour and more behind time, would you

14

reckon, and I'm the one expected to pull it all back, rein it in just like it was everyday and roll this outfit into Rainwater like nothin' had happened. That's what I'm expected to do, Moose. You hearin' me there?'

Moose was hearing him sure enough above the beat of driven hoofs, the crack and strain of tack, grind of wheels and protesting timbers, but knew better than to fuel an already glowing fire.

'And for why are we all this time late?' Charlie continued undeterred by Moose's silence. 'Well, I'll tell you for why: because some two-bit stinkin', sonofabitch gamblin' man with a whole sight more of a loose head than sense, gets himself into a hand of poker with Eli Carney's wife as the pot. Can you credit that, Moose? Dora Carney is the stake. And then, hell, the fella plays the hand full out, wins and tells Eli he can keep his wife. Meantime . . . Yeah, well, I've said all that.'

He had, thought Moose, and doubt-less would a hundred times again before they ever saw Rainwater.

'What I ain't said,' Charlie went on, 'is how with that Willard Pierce breathin' time-keepin' down our necks every goddamn chance he gets, we'd better watch to it, keep our heads and our tempers and not let him rile us no more than is natural to his type. In other words, Moose, do your best to ignore him. And that wife of his. She'll be spreadin' herself thick as molasses before we hit the desert, you mark my words. Yessir. I tell you, Moose, there's somethin' about this run as ain't right. Don't feel right. Don't smell right. You get that feelin'?'

Moose merely grunted and nodded and cradled his Winchester like it was a newborn. If Charlie felt something was not right, then it must be so. Charlie was never wrong on that count. Not ever.

# 3

Of the five passengers boarding the stage that afternoon, four had quickly assigned themselves to the much prized corner seats: Madelaine Pierce with her back to the team facing her husband; Frank Holden facing Mr Jones, which had left Lemuel Buthnott with the choice of a middle seat facing either way. He had chosen, not surprisingly, to sit with an uninterrupted view of Mrs Pierce.

Charlie Deakin had driven the outfit less than a mile clear of town when Willard Pierce consulted his timepiece, appeared to make a mental note of the hour and then fix his angry gaze on the apparently sleeping Mr Jones.

'And now, sir,' he began, as if about to chair a stockholders' meeting, 'seeing as we are finally underway, perhaps you will be so kind as to offer your apologies for the delay. I would deem it the least you can do.'

There was no answer.

'Mr Jones,' persisted the banker, 'I am addressing you, sir. Please extend me the courtesy of some attention.' Again, no answer.

Pierce snorted and waited a moment before continuing, 'You, sir, are by far and away one of the most ill-mannered men it has been my misfortune to encounter — if not *the* most. Not only do you delay the departure of the stage on its scheduled run with some ridiculous story of playing a hand of poker in which another man's wife is the stake, you then have the temerity to sit there, seemingly asleep, and make not the slightest effort towards an apology for not only the time you have wasted — for myself, my wife and your fellow passengers — but also the considerable inconvenience and stress you have so thoughtlessly and to my mind needlessly inflicted. I, for one, shall not be letting the matter rest nor permit the incident to go unnoticed by those — '

'You all through, mister?' muttered Jones from beneath the hat covering his face.

'I beg your pardon?' growled Pierce.

'I said are you all through, or are you goin' to keep up that washerwoman's cackle all the way to Bloodrock?'

'Washerwoman's cackle — how dare you, sir! How dare you have the gall — '

Jones pushed the hat from his face, sat fully upright and turned the dark stare directly into the banker's eyes. 'Mister, I don't give a whore's bad breath about you or anybody else for that matter. I'm on this stage simply to get to Rainwater. Now if you persist in mouthin' like we've just heard, I'm goin' to have to come across there and shut you right up. You got that? You hearin' me?'

Willard Pierce did not move. He could only blink and feel his mouth drying to dust. Madelaine Pierce dabbed the lace-fringed handkerchief carefully across her neck and into her cleavage. Lemuel Buthnott swallowed twice in quick succession. Frank Holden gazed out of the window space and watched the world go by.

★ ★ ★

It was full dark, the moon high, the stars bright, the air balmy with the day's heat when Charlie swung the stage to the glow of the welcoming lantern lights at the station at Bloodrock. Thake Todd, the station's long-serving manager, and his wife Clarissa were on the home veranda as usual to greet the arrivals.

'Runnin' a whole lot behind time, ain't you, Charlie?' called Thake as he crossed to the outfit now halted close to the porch. 'You had trouble or somethin'?'

'Tell you later,' said Charlie. 'Supper up, Clarissa?' he smiled, climbing down from his seat.

'Meat pie and apple to follow, just

the way you like it, Charlie,' grinned the woman, running her hands through the apron at her waist.

'Ain't nobody bakes a better pie south of the Rockies,' said Moose, already smacking his lips at the prospect.

'Get away with you, Moose Topper,' said Clarissa. 'You ain't foolin' me none. Your portion'll be the same as the others.'

'See to the folks, will you, Thake?' gestured Charlie. 'We got five aboard. One lady — Mrs Pierce. You know of her, eh? Willard Pierce's wife.'

Thake nodded, winked and tapped the side of his nose. 'Got you, Charlie. You bet to it.'

A half-hour later, with the passengers seated round Clarissa's ample kitchen table where an array of food, including the much famed meat pie, had been arranged, Thake drew Charlie aside to the shadowed end of the veranda.

'That Mr Jones,' he murmured so softly it was barely more than a whisper. 'I seen his face before. It's kinda familiar.'

'Where?' asked Charlie, one eye on the open door to the living area. 'Here, at the station? He been through here before?'

'No, not here,' hissed Thake. 'Some place else. Can't quite recall, leastways not yet, I can't. But I will, I will.' He came closer. 'Tell you somethin', though, he ain't no Mr Jones. Nossir, he ain't. That face didn't ever answer to the name Jones. I'd swear to that . . . '

★　★　★

Passengers making the journey by stage from Harper's Town to Rainwater had completed the shortest part of the haul by the time they arrived at Bloodrock for the first of the two overnight stays necessary to reach their final destination.

The station had been carefully sited only two miles short of the sometimes perilous but always arduous trail across the miles of open desert still referred to by many as the 'badlands' that had to be crossed before reaching the second stop station at Needlepoint. It was, as Charlie Deakin was prone to remark on many occasions, a 'dog's backside of a crossing'. Heat, dirt, dust and a sun that seemed intent on scorching to near death everything it could see, were only the start of it. 'Then there's the outlaws, the two-bit drifters, the scumbags who get holed up there 'cus there ain't no place else to hide.'

Charlie and Moose were always more than relieved when they saw that first twist of smoke from the stack at the Needlepoint Station.

Hence the siting at Bloodrock where passengers were guaranteed the best of traditional homestead cooking, root beer, a good night's sleep between clean linen sheets in beds furnished with the finest mattresses, and as hearty a breakfast as they wished before embarking on the desert crossing.

Clarissa Todd had built and established a fine reputation stretching the length and breadth of the territory for her standard of service and hospitality, whilst Thake was, in Charlie Deakin's opinion, 'second-to-none' when it came to station management.

Bloodrock, it was said, was your last chance to taste and feel clean and decent for a very long way.

This night, the passengers having partaken of Clarissa's generous supper — they had eaten for the most part in silence — had retired to their separate rooms early, leaving only Frank Holden on the veranda where he contemplated the night and smoked a last cheroot before he too made his way to his bed.

Charlie, Moose and Thake had come together after finishing separate suppers, to drink root beer and sample the permitted single measure of Thake's best whiskey, and, of course, to talk. Normally these conversations were of happenings in Harper's Town and Rainwater which Charlie and his partner had either witnessed or heard tell of.

But tonight was different. Tonight, Thake was anxious with other, more important news.

'I've remembered,' he said in a low, careful tone when the three of them were settled on the porch in the soft glow of lantern light. 'Knew I would sooner or later. Like I said, he ain't no Jones. That's mebbe his travellin' name. His real name is Bone. John Bone. More commonly known as Denver Bone on account of how he used to work out of Denver. That's where he made his name. He's a gunslinger, Charlie, an out-and-out gunslinger and a whole sight more, you can bet. *And* he's got a price on his head. That's where I seen his face — on a poster at the sheriff's office time I was visitin' Ford Town.'

'How long back is that?' asked Moose.

'Hell, must be a couple, mebbe nearer three years back. He was wanted for a killin' out at Ridgesands and another at Annie's Town. Yessir . . . John 'Denver' Bone . . . can see his face now, clear as the moon up there. That's him, all right, that's your Mr Jones. You're cartin' a whole heap of trouble there, Charlie. Best watch your back.'

* * *

Charlie had every intention of watching his back, and not only because of Mr Jones, or Denver Bone as he now appeared to be. He had been troubled since the very start of the run. Jones was never going to be easy to handle, Willard Pierce still more so. If Holden kept to himself, as he seemed to be doing, and Buthnott occupied himself with his ogling of Madelaine Pierce, that would do just fine.

But unfortunately Mrs Pierce, Charlie suspected, was not cut out for the quiet, unobtrusive life. She was the flame and it was only a matter of time now before the moths were on the wing around her.

# 4

'Darn me if he ain't worse than a burst blister in a bad fittin' boot and then some!' Thake Todd paced the length of the long stabling at the Bloodrock Station, turned and paced back to where Charlie Deakin and Moose Topper waited for him to simmer down. 'Know what, Willard-all-important-Pierce ain't stopped askin' me since sun-up for a precise timetable of the run across the desert. Wants to know where the stage will be at such-and-such a time; where it'll be a half-hour later; when it will be here, when it'll be there. Got himself a whole detailed map of the area. Man's nothin' but a sore head on a lousy day. If he spent as much time lookin' to that young wife of his, we'd all be a whole lot happier.'

'That's Willard Pierce for you,' said Moose, smacking his lips and rolling his eyes. 'And we've got him all the way to Rainwater.'

'You're welcome to him,' groaned Thake. 'Let's hope he plans a long stay!'

'Why would he want a map of the territory and why, specifically, the desert?' asked Charlie, rubbing his chin as his gaze roved over the already brightening early morning. 'Either of you figured that?'

Moose shrugged. 'Beats me,' he said. 'But then the man ain't natural, is he? I mean, he don't think like you and me, does he? Don't even seem to think about his wife, and most fellas'd find that pretty difficult not to do, her bein' the looker she is.'

'I'll tell you why he's got a map,' snapped Thake, clearing the sweat from his brow with a large bandanna. 'It's because he's out of his mind with this business of time. Can't leave it alone, like it was some big itch. Just has to keep on scratchin' it. Hell, what does it matter what time the stage gets anywhere, f'Chris'sake! It'll be there when it gets there, won't it? World ain't goin' to stop spinnin' for a minute here, a minute there. Type like Pierce will be timin' out his last breath when it comes, and doubtless warnin' his Maker not to be late takin' him!'

Thake spat. Moose nodded. Charlie's gaze moved on, his eyes narrowing on the jumble of thoughts scudding through his head.

'Well, guess we'd better go see if them folk are ready for boardin',' said Thake at last, taking a deep breath. 'See you fellas on the return, eh? But don't bring Willard Pierce!'

★ ★ ★

'I always think this is the worse part of the journey, Mrs Pierce. Don't you agree?' Lemuel Buthnott swayed to the motion of the stage as the pace quickened out of Bloodrock, and smiled softly at the woman seated in the corner. His eyes strayed a moment to the still ample exposure of cleavage, then settled on her face.

'This is my first crossing of the desert,' said Madelaine Pierce, clearing a speck of dust from her cheek. 'I have yet to pass judgement on the experience.' Her smile did nothing to discourage Buthnott's busy eyes.

'Quite so, ma'am,' said the store-keeper. 'I, of course, make the journey annually. The years have not improved the discomforts of this particular part of the trail. What with the heat, the dust, the flies — '

'How long before we are half-way across?' blurted Pierce, consulting his folded map. 'Given we maintain this pace,' he added.

'Well,' began Buthnott, stretching to see out of the stage, 'if memory serves me well — '

'At this pace we'll be half-way across in two-and-a-half hours,' said Holden from his corner seat.

'You are familiar with the territory, sir?' asked Pierce.

'Some. I've crossed before, usually ridin' alone.'

Jones's dark stare strayed from the landscape to Holden.

'I didn't catch your line of business, Mr Holden,' said Pierce.

'Didn't name it. And it don't matter, anyhow.'

'As you wish,' said Pierce, consulting his time-piece. 'By my reckonin', the driver has made up some twenty-seven minutes.'

'Well, ain't that just dandy!' grinned Jones. 'A whole twenty-seven minutes! Who'd have figured it, eh?'

The colour rose in Pierce's cheeks. Holden turned his gaze back to the sprawl of sand and the shimmer of the distant horizon. Madelaine Pierce produced a fresh lace handkerchief, heavily perfumed, and dabbed at her neck and cleavage.

'I'm sure Mr Holden is right,' mumbled Buthnott. 'Two-and-a-half hours sounds about right at this pace, of course.' He smiled and went back to

31

watching Mrs Pierce.

Jones released a deep belch without apology and studied Pierce's examination of the map. He was about to say something to the banker, then changed his mind. The fellow's wife was a much more interesting diversion.

★　★　★

Charlie Deakin spat a mouthful of dirt clear of the whip of the searing wind across his face and urged the team forward.

'Sooner we're clear of this sand the better,' he called to Moose. 'Never did like it, never will. Sight of Needlepoint can't never come too soon in my book. What'd you reckon, Moose? You ain't much for sand, are you?'

Moose was a while before he answered, then said, 'Well, I ain't reckonin' to it right now, Charlie. I got my eye on somethin' I ain't never seen before, not out here, anyhow, and it ain't goin' away.'

'Hey, you ain't for spookin' me more than I already am, are you, Moose? Hell, what with Thake tellin' me as how Mr Jones ain't who he's supposed to be — like as not he's some scumbag gunslinger — and Willard Pierce sittin' back there with that darned timepiece in his hand, and his wife showin' herself to just about any fool male eyes happenin' to cross her, and runnin' late and the heat and sand . . . I ain't much for bein' messed with, and that's the truth of it.' Charlie cracked the reins and tightened his grip on the leather. 'So what you seen? Where?'

'Out there in them rocks at the outcrop,' said Moose, indicating the shadowed mass away to the east. 'I call them the cookies on account as how they remind me of how my old ma's cookies always turned out! Kinda like big bears on their backs.'

'Yeah, yeah, I see the rocks. Seen them a hundred times, ain't I? So what's so different today?'

'I ain't exactly sure,' pondered

Moose, his eyes narrowing. 'It's like there's somethin' out there as keeps glintin'.'

'Glintin'? You mean like the sun glintin' on a gun barrel? Hell, that's all we need!'

'Or somebody with a mirror.'

Charlie cracked the reins again and urged the team on. 'Now what in tarnation would somebody be doin' out there with a mirror, f'Chris'sake?'

'Signallin'.'

'Signallin' to who . . . Oh, my God! You mean signallin' to somebody aboard the stage?'

'Well, there ain't nobody else out here to my reckonin', is there? So if it ain't to us, then it ain't to nobody, 'cus there ain't nobody.' Moose adjusted the spread of the rifle across his knees. 'What you goin' to do?'

'I'll tell you what I ain't goin' to do. I ain't goin' chasin' hell-bent to find out who might or might not be out there. Nossir, I ain't for takin' that risk, not to mention losin' still more time.'

'So?' asked Moose.

'So we push right on and trust this team of ours will get us through to Needlepoint in one piece — and *on time*!'

★ ★ ★

'You find the landscape interesting, Mr Holden?' Willard Pierce settled a steady gaze on the man's face.

'Fascinatin',' said Holden, his concentration tight on the passing scene. Pierce studied the man intently for a moment. 'But you've seen it before, as you've already told us.'

Holden's gaze wandered to the banker. 'It's one thing on a horse, another in a stage.'

'And which do you prefer?' smiled Pierce. 'For myself, I think the comforts of the stage, albeit limited and somewhat sparse, far outweigh horseback and a bedroll. But, then, that would probably depend on your mission, wouldn't it?'

'I'm for the stage,' said Buthnott without shifting his eyes from Madelaine Pierce. 'There's so much more to see from the stage.'

Jones grunted from beneath his hat. Holden made no comment.

'They do say, of course,' continued Pierce, 'that it takes a special sort of man to survive alone out there. It's no place for the fearful, or so I'm told. In fact, I've heard it said there are as many human skulls and bones out there as there are rocks. An exaggeration perhaps, but it illustrates the severity of the place.' He consulted his timepiece. 'Three days maximum is a man's lifespan without water — or once again, so I'm told.'

Madelaine Pierce stifled a soft shudder and adjusted the neckline of her dress. Buthnott leaned forward on the pretext of the sway of the stage. Holden paid the banker no attention.

'Seems to me like you spend an awful lot of time listenin' to what folks get to tellin' you,' muttered Jones from beneath his hat. 'That's a habit that can get to be dangerous. You should watch it, fella.'

Pierce began to fume, then to sneer, but buried both in a deep sigh. 'I'm beginning to find you a very sad person, Mr Jones. You appear not to have the capacity to listen, therefore none to learn of the value of experience, even when it is that of others. You should try'

'Well, here's an experience movin' in right now,' said Holden, craning forward to the window space. 'Riders comin' at a pace that means they're headin' only one place.'

Willard Pierce consulted his time-piece and smiled.

# 5

At first they came in a cloud of swirling dust and flying dirt. They veered from the outcrop to a direct line for the stage as grey blurred shapes, until the blurs had a form and became recognizable.

'Riders!' yelled Moose. 'And they don't look none too friendly. We're goin' to be hit!'

Now the thundering beat of hoofs, snorts, rapid jangling of tack and creaks of leather seemed to drown even the groaning of the stage as Charlie whipped up the team to a faster pace.

'How many?' he shouted, glancing anxiously at Moose.

'Hard to say at this distance, but there's plenty.' Moose wiped the dust from his eyes. 'We makin' a run for it?'

'We'll try.'

The team strained, the stage bounced, crashed back to four safe wheels, swung to the left, straightened and rolled on creakily.

'I can count a dozen, mebbe more,' yelled Moose again, straining his eyes to pierce the dust and shimmering heat-haze. 'Fifteen,' he added seconds later, then: 'Hell, make that twenty!'

'Who are they, f'Chris'sake?'

'No idea, but them I can see sure look mean.'

Charlie whooped encouragement to the team and strained his every muscle for control of the reins. Thankfully, the going here was good, a solid packing of baked sand that formed the so-called main trail, but there were snags ahead as he knew well enough. Soon the packed sand would give way to softer, drifting flows where the surface was never the same two days running, then would come the stones, small rocks and finally boulders, many of them hidden as the desert winds whipped the sands to ever changing shapes and levels.

'Now what you seein'?' called Charlie above the continuing groans and creaks of the stage and the beat of hoofs.

'They're breakin' to two lots, one to the left, one to the right.'

'Comin' at us on both sides.'

'You got it, Charlie. And they're comin' fast. You want I should fire a warnin' shot?'

'Hell, no, we ain't askin' to be bushwhacked. We'll hold this pace 'til we're forced to slow, then . . . God knows!'

The stage bounced again, threatened to slither to the left, righted itself in a groaning slide and bounced again. Charlie figured for his passengers having a really rough ride! How many times had Mrs Pierce bounced clear into Buthnott's waiting arms? Not often enough, he would wager!

'Heck, Charlie, they've drawn rifles,' yelled Moose. 'You're goin' to have to haul up. If them rats out there get to shootin' . . . '

The crack of the first shot rose above all other sounds. A second whined only inches above the roof of the stage. The third, from closer range as the leading riders gained on the now wild-eyed team, hit Moose Topper clean through the heart and toppled him from the stage to the dirt like a crumpled ball of paper blown on the wind.

'Moose!' screamed Charlie at the top of his voice as he dared to look back at the body sprawled on the trail. 'Moose, f'Chris'sake! Moose!'

But there was no movement from the dark shape now far behind him and the only sounds filling his ears were of pounding hoofs, protesting timbers and from somewhere the shouts of a man to rein up and to do it right now if he wanted to live.

Charlie rolled the stage to a halt and let the tears flow freely down his burning cheeks.

\* \* \*

'Get down! Now! Real easy.'

The order was barked from behind the levelled barrel of a Winchester by a man with glinting eyes set in a mahogany tanned face with a scar on his right cheek that twisted his grin to a wet-lipped sneer.

Charlie, the tears having dried to a fiery anger that seemed to be burning a hole in his stomach, did as he was ordered, stepped to the sand and raised his arms. He gazed over the faces of the watching men.

Scumbag gunslingers of just about the lowest kind, he reckoned. The dregs of every two-bit town between here and the seaboard in any direction. A filthy, smelly, dust smothered bunch that would gun a man down without giving it a second thought. Just like they had Moose Topper. Killed in cold blood.

Charlie bit back a sudden surge of anger, a desperate longing to spit in the face of the man who had barked the order, and swallowed.

Who were they, he wondered? Where had they come from? Why had they been here at precisely this time as if waiting on the stage to pass through?

'Open up the stage there, let's see what we've got,' ordered the man with the scar.

Charlie sighed and closed his eyes. He could already see and hear what was coming.

First down was Lemuel Buthnott, his face crimson, sweat-lathered and gleaming, his eyes swimming like bullhead fish. His hands were shaking. In fact, his whole body was quivering. He swallowed and tried desperately to find his voice.

'I'm . . . I'm *the* Buthnott of Buthnott's mercantile back there . . . back there in Harper's Town . . . Sole proprietor . . . and I just . . . I just want to say . . . to say as how . . . ' The voice trailed away for a moment. Sweat dripped from the man's face. 'As how,' he began again, 'I'm not without means and would be happy . . . happy to offer whatever you . . . ' The voice croaked into oblivion. Buthnott closed his eyes and moved his lips as if in silent prayer.

The riders tittered among themselves.

Scarface spat. 'Stand aside, mister, and don't go messin' them nice creased pants you're wearin'!'

The riders tittered again, wiped their faces, scratched, fidgeted and waited.

Mr Jones was the next to appear, his gunbelt and holstered Colt already in his hand. 'Figured you'd be strippin' me of this, so thought I'd save you the trouble,' he said flatly, as he threw down the belt. His dark stare settled like a sudden shadow on the scarred man's face.

'Darn sure I've seen him before, boss,' said one of the riders narrowing his gaze. 'Kinda looks familiar. I seen you some place before, fella?'

'Not so,' said Jones, without looking at the man. 'I'd have remembered a mug as ugly as yours.'

The rider drew a gun, his teeth gritted in a snarl. The scarred man raised an arm. 'Not yet, Lew. Just wait. Time will come.'

Frank Holden was the next to be framed in the doorway of the stage. He merely screwed his eyes against the fierce glare of the sun, ran a dismissive gaze over the faces of the riders and stepped down with a sigh that might have seemed like relief.

'Hot,' he said through a slow smile. 'Definitely hot.'

The scarface leader of the bunch tightened the rein on his mount as it tossed its head against the heat and pestering flies. 'And just who might you be, mister?' he growled.

'Me?' said Holden. 'Oh, I'm nobody. Just passin' through, Harper's Town to Rainwater. Name's Holden — Frank Holden.'

Scarface steadied his stare on the man's face. 'What line of business?' he growled again.

'This and that,' shrugged Holden, his smile broadening. 'What I can find, where I can find it. Nothin' special right now.'

'A con man,' grinned one of the

45

riders. 'Charm the pants off a Bible-pusher.'

'More like the clothes off a woman!' chimed another.

The riders laughed, shifted to the fidgeting of their mounts, spat, ran grubby hands over grubby faces then fell to a silence in which nothing moved and not a breath could be heard as Madelaine Pierce appeared in the doorway, accepted Holden's hand to support her to the ground and swished her skirts about her with an air of disdain and anger.

'I hope you men know what you are doing and precisely who it is you are dealing with here,' she said, the skirts swishing again across the sand, her eyes flashing like jewels.

The riders watched, enthralled; one man swallowed noisily, another narrowed his eyes, his imagination running wild, the rider at his side licked his lips.

'Oh, yes, ma'am, you can bet to that,' smiled Scarface, tipping the brim of his hat. 'It's a pleasure to meet you, Mrs Pierce.'

'You know who I am?' frowned the woman, her expression softening instantly.

'Yes, indeed, ma'am. Know you and the gentleman lucky enough to be your husband.'

'Ah, Mr Coe,' beamed Willard Pierce, appearing at the open door, his timepiece in his hand. 'And as near on time as makes little odds considering the inefficiency of this line.' He pocketed the timepiece and gazed back along the trail. 'A fatality I see. You had to shoot the man?'

' 'Fraid so, sir,' said Scarface. 'Necessary in order to halt the stage in one piece and to save you and your good lady here any further discomfort.'

'Of course, of course,' said Pierce with a wave of his hand as he stepped down. 'Perfectly understandable in the circumstances.'

'Willard!' flared his wife, the colour

rising in her cheeks. 'That is Moose Topper back there. These men shot him in cold blood. You cannot possibly — '

'Be quiet, woman!'

Madelaine Pierce stood open-mouthed, silent, bewildered under the stare of her husband as he turned to face her.

'Not another sound from you,' he ordered, the stare deepening. 'Not unless you wish me to feed you to these woman-hungry men here who would, I am sure, be most happy to curb your impetuosity. Do I make myself clear?'

The woman's face paled visibly. A trickle of cold sweat swam into her cleavage. Buthnott's face erupted as if doused in a water trough. Jones flared his nostrils and shifted his weight from one hip to the other. Frank Holden narrowed his gaze on the banker's face. Charlie Deakin mouthed words and curses that set his stubble alight with beads of sweat.

'And now, Mr Coe,' resumed Pierce, turning to Scarface, 'if you and your men are ready we will get on with this and take our leave as quickly as possible.'

'Yessir!' said Coe, reining his mount to face the riders. 'Get to it, boys.'

# 6

A handful of men dismounted and began to take charge of the stage to an obviously well-rehearsed pattern. One man concentrated on the team and an inspection of the tack; a second man climbed into the stage and began a systematic search of the interior; two men concerned themselves solely with the luggage and the contents of the trunks, valises and cases; a fifth man checked over the timbers; a sixth squatted to examine the state of the wheels.

No one spoke, no one moved. They could only watch, Buthnott in a steadily perspiring state of near collapse, Jones with a look of resigned amusement in the smirk at his lips. Frank Holden missed nothing, his eyes seeming to observe every detail of the operation and the faces of the men carrying it out. Coe and Willard Pierce watched with satisfaction. Madelaine Pierce was too bewildered to move, let alone speak.

It was Charlie Deakin who finally broke the silence. 'You ain't got no right to go messin' with that outfit like you are. It's company property and in my direct charge.'

'Wrong, Mr Deakin,' smiled Pierce. 'That outfit, as you put it, is now my property. I am taking it and all its contents from you.' He gazed over the faces of the passengers with a suddenly chilled glaze to his look. 'You will do well, all of you, to consider yourselves fortunate not to be lying dead in the dirt. I am sparing your lives, but only for what, I am sure, will be a fleeting passage of time or for as long as you will be able to survive out here without so much as a canteen of water between you.'

'Willard,' muttered his wife, the sweat beading freely on her exposed flesh, 'will you please, please tell me what in heaven's name is going on here? Have you lost your mind completely?'

'Not at all, my dear,' said the banker, thrusting his hands behind his back. 'This is merely part one of a plan I have been devising, honing and finally putting into action over a period of many months. You see, the bank back there in Harper's Town has for some time been facing a — shall we say — shortage of funds to meet its commitments and obligations. In other words, my dear, in little short of a year it will have nothing and be worthless — as will I along with it.'

'But — ' began the woman, her eyes in a torment of tears and amazement.

Pierce held up a hand, and continued, 'I have no intention of spending my declining years in abject poverty. I have therefore, over time, been *transferring*, shall we say, the assets of the bank money, bonds, etc to a safer place where, once south of the border, I shall retire in peace and plenty for the rest of my days — unavailable, as it were, to my creditors and to all intents and purposes lost to civilization.'

Madelaine Pierce ran a hand across her eyes, all pretence of appearances now dismissed. 'But what about me? I'm your wife, damnit!'

'You, my dear, are the woman who has gladly partaken of my wealth and position with relish and given precisely nothing back! I found you with no more than the clothes you stood in, and that is how I am leaving you. You can go to Hell and there taunt and tempt all the men of the Devil's making you please, just as you have in Harper's Town since the day I so foolishly married you. To Hell, Madelaine, you deserve it!'

'What happens now, Pierce?' clipped Holden. 'You leavin' us and pullin' out, taking the stage, the luggage, everythin'?'

'Precisely that, Mr Holden,' grinned Pierce consulting his timepiece. 'In exactly ten minutes if Mr Coe is satisfied that all is as it should be.'

'You got it, Mr Pierce,' said Coe. 'Ten minutes it is.'

'Precision, you see,' smiled Pierce, pocketing the timepiece. 'I like precision and keeping to time. Vital in an operation of this nature.'

'You ain't never goin' to get away with it,' groaned Charlie through an already parched throat. 'Not if I have to hunt you for a lifetime. You put good note to that, Pierce, you hear?'

The banker adjusted the set of his coat. 'I hear you well enough, Mr Deakin, but I somehow doubt your ability to fulfil the promise. Mr Coe here, who has so faithfully and reliably been instrumental in enabling me to come this far with my plan, assures me that few men can survive more than three days out here, as I am sure you yourself are well aware. Three days from now I shall be making my final preparations to cross the border for the very last time. You, Mr Deakin, will be in the throes of a painful death.' His smile thickened. 'I fancy I have the advantage.'

'You're a sonofabitch, Willard Pierce!'

54

cursed the woman.

'And you, my dear, are what you have always been — a cheap and rather nasty whore.' Pierce turned to Coe. 'Let's be gone, my friend. This place is beginning to smell!'

\* \* \*

It was ten minutes to the second when the man deputed to drive the stage on to its destination was given the order to pull out.

Willard Pierce, seated alone in the coach with Coe, did not look back as the outfit flanked by riders, some trailing loose-lined mounts, creaked, jangled, strained and finally groaned into life and was soon no more than a fading cloud of dust heading to the shimmer of a distant horizon.

Madelaine Pierce, her clenched fists pounding the air, screamed at the top of her voice until the sweat glowed on her face and her eyes were burning as fierce as hot coals.

'You got that out of your system, ma'am?' clipped Jones when the woman was still and silent again. She simply glared at him then looked away to the still fading cloud of dust. 'I'll take that as a 'Yes',' added Jones. 'Good. Now get yourself straightened up. There ain't goin' to be no place here for hysterics.'

'That's easy for you to say,' flared the woman, wiping a hand across her cheek. 'You haven't — '

'T'ain't easy for anybody, lady,' snapped Jones. 'And it's goin' to get a whole sight worse unless we think straight and get organized.'

'He's right, ma'am,' said Charlie. 'What's happened here in the last hour ain't nothin' short of . . . Hell, there ain't no words for it. But we're as we are and if we're goin' to survive — '

'There's very little chance of that, surely, is there?' said Buthnott, removing his jacket before mopping an already soaked bandanna round his neck. 'As I see it — '

Jones raised a hand to silence the

storekeeper, then turned to Holden. 'What do you reckon, mister? You got any figurin' on this?'

Holden shielded his eyes against the glare and shimmer and scanned the horizon in all directions. 'Way I see it right now, we got only one choice. There's somethin' like what appears to be a hill range to the north-east. Hell of a trek, but if we could make it that far, well, who knows we might get lucky and find a homesteader with horses, or mebbe meet up with travellers. Facts are: we can't walk the distance to the station at Needlepoint, so them hills, however far, whatever they hold, are all we've got. You know the territory, Mr Deakin, what we got out there?'

Charlie's gaze had been concentrated on Jones, or Denver Bone as he was now coming to think of him, for the past minute, his thoughts spinning at the prospects of how a man like Bone would handle the situation. Survival for himself at any price, or would he —

'Mr Deakin,' prompted Holden breaking Charlie's concentration.

'Oh, yes, sorry,' said Charlie. 'The hills. Fair distance away. A long, long walk, specially in these conditions and, right now, not a spoonful of water between us.'

'Any way we can solve that?' asked Jones.

Charlie shielded his eyes to scan the land to the north-east. 'There's a gulch and a creek some ten miles south of the hills. I've known the water pools there to be full this time of year. Other times . . . dry as dust. But it's worth a try. If we move now, fix a steady pace and hold to it and forget about feelin' thirsty we could make the gulch late nightfall; the hills in two days, three at most.'

'And then?' murmured Madelaine Pierce.

'We'll find whatever we find, lady,' clipped Jones. 'Right — are we agreed? We walk?'

'While we're still standin' and able,' said Holden.

'Hold it,' interrupted Charlie. 'There's Moose back there. I ain't leavin' him for no buzzard meat.'

Jones grunted. 'Do whatever you can,' he ordered brusquely. 'But make it fast. We need to get goin'.'

The group moved away towards the body of Moose Topper where it lay dark and lifeless as rock back down the trail.

Buthnott shuffled to Madelaine Pierce's side. 'Would you mind if I walked with you, Mrs Pierce?' he asked tentatively.

The woman gave him a quick, flushed glance. 'If you must, Mr Buthnott,' she answered.

Buthnott smiled and fell to her pace. 'I can't say how I feel for you, Mrs Pierce,' he murmured. 'I mean regarding your husband and what he's done. I had no idea, none at all. I'm sure no one else did. And to think we were all living there in Harper's Town. Neighbours practically. It hardly bears — '

'I'd rather not discuss it, Mr

59

Buthnott.' Her glance was fierce. 'Let's concentrate on survival, shall we?'

Buthnott smiled softly to himself and eased just a fraction closer to the woman's side.

# 7

Charlie Deakin, bringing up the rear of the column of five that finally began the long walk to the hills, had been the last to leave the spot where they had buried Moose.

They had scooped out a shallow grave with their hands, lowered Moose's body into it and covered it best they could with sand and the few rocks and stones to hand. Charlie had bared his head, gestured for the others to do likewise, and said a few words over his lifelong friend and partner, praying quietly that he might have a safe journey to wherever his Maker might be taking him. Then he had waited while the others filed away and fell to Jones's brisk orders.

When at last he turned the column was already moving, its destination a direct line ahead to the gulch and their hope — their only hope — of finding water.

Jones had chosen to lead and set the pace, with Madelaine Pierce following, Buthnott on her heels, and Holden moving silently but watchfully ahead of Charlie.

Last in the line was no bad place to be, Charlie reckoned, as he tipped his hat against the glare, took a deep breath and fell to the pace. He would sooner be watching his passengers — motley lot as they were, and maybe soon to get desperate with it — than have them watching him, specially Mr Jones. No saying to what might be going through his mind right now, but whatever it would be fathomed to bring him out on top.

They had gone less than a couple of miles when Holden dropped back to walk alongside Charlie.

'How long before the stage company put out a search for us, Mr Deakin?'

Charlie considered for a moment. 'When we don't show tonight at

Needlepoint, they'll wait mebbe four, five hours. By then we'll either have gotten lucky at the gulch or be facin' certain death. Half a day's delay at best is company policy.'

'And then?' asked Holden.

'Then they'll mount up a party at Harper's Town and wire through to Rainwater. My bettin' would be Sheriff Maguire will head a full posse from town.'

'They likely to find us?'

Charlie wiped sweat from his brow. 'They'll pick up our tracks, that's for sure. I'd reckon for Maguire splittin' his party one half to follow the stage tracks, one half to follow us. What we don't need is a sandstorm. We get a wind out here this time of year and tracks disappear like spit on a hot rock.'

Holden walked on in silence for a while. 'What do you reckon Pierce will do with the stage?' he said, wringing out his bandanna for the third time since the group had set off.

Charlie grinned. 'I'll tell you what he

ain't goin' to do. He sure as hell ain't goin' to roll it into Rainwater or any other two-bit border town. No, he'll set the team free and burn the stage somewhere up there in them hills. Any number of places you can do that. Way I read it, that sonofabitch sidekick Coe's been organizin' things behind the scenes for weeks. There'll be fresh horses, fresh water, all the comforts waitin' on Pierce as he scoops his loot and crosses the border.'

'And where do you reckon he'll do that, Mr Deakin?'

'I'm workin' on it, Mr Holden. Workin' on it hard. But it's got to be somewhere close to where he's got his money stashed and waitin' on collection. And that's mebbe narrowin' the field some.'

They fell to silence again and trudged on through the searing heat, the sun still high and fierce.

Charlie waited his moment, then said, 'You crossed that fella Jones before?'

Holden was in no hurry to respond. 'Why do you ask?' he said carefully. 'Have you?'

'Well, it's kinda strange,' shrugged Charlie, laying his bait with as much conviction as he could summon, 'but there's somethin' about him, somethin' about that face . . . ' His voice tailed away as he glanced expectantly at Holden. 'Somethin' I kinda figure I've seen before,' he added hurriedly.

Holden adjusted the set of his hat. 'You could be right, Mr Deakin. Had the same feelin' back there in town. But when, where, and just who the fella is, well, there's a mystery for you.'

Holden trudged ahead to his place at the back of Buthnott and resumed the steady pace.

★ ★ ★

They had walked for almost two hours when Jones called a halt and said they should rest for a while.

Buthnott and Madelaine Pierce sank

to the sand breathless, sweat-soaked and near exhausted. 'But no sleepin',' Jones ordered, glancing anxiously at the woman.

Holden stood aside scanning the horizon from left to right and back again in a regular sweep, as if expecting riders to break through the shimmering heat haze at any moment.

'I don't doubt friend Coe and his boys will be back,' quipped Jones, coming to Holden's side. 'They're long gone for now and mebbe ratin' us for buzzard meat, but they're goin' to have to be sure. You reckon?'

Holden continued his steady scanning. 'Mebbe so,' he murmured. 'But there'll be others out there sooner or later. A stage don't just disappear without somebody gettin' to query it.'

Jones spat fiercely into the sand. 'Well, I wouldn't set too much store by it myself. Desert's an awful big place and we're in it, up to our necks.' He called across to Charlie. 'How we doin', Mr Deakin? Keepin' to time?'

'Just about,' answered Charlie, 'but we can't afford to slow the pace. Dark comes down real fast. We've got to be at the gulch by nightfall, otherwise . . . Yeah, well, we won't contemplate that.'

'No, Mr Deakin, we won't,' said Jones.

'I'm not sure I can go on,' said the woman suddenly, her face awash with sweat and the first burns of blistering. 'I think I'm all in.'

'Nonsense,' soothed Buthnott, laying a hand on her arm. 'You mustn't think like that, Mrs Pierce. If we give in this early — '

'It's all very well for you, all of you,' she snapped, her eyes gleaming. 'You haven't lost everything. I've no home, no money, no clothes, no damned husband and no hope! I might as well quit right now. Get it over with. You can leave me here, go on without me.'

Jones's glare had darkened. 'You want I should step over there right now, lady, and strangle you with my bare hands, save you the agony of dyin' of thirst? You want I should do that? Believe me I could and I would, but it ain't goin' to happen.' He fixed his thumbs in the belt of his pants and tightened his glare. 'I couldn't give a dog's dinner for your husband, what he's done or what he's plannin' to do. All I do know is he could have had that rat Coe and his boys shoot the hell out of us back there and left us for dead in the dirt. But he didn't. He figured for us dyin' anyhow. And that was his big mistake, 'cus I ain't got no intention of doin' any such thing, not this side of that gulch and them hills. And you're comin' right along of me, Mrs Pierce, same as the others.'

Jones crossed to the woman, stood over her and offered her a hand. 'Get to your feet, lady, and walk!'

★ ★ ★

'Know somethin',' said Charlie, relishing the first cool of the day as the sun sank low in the West and Holden dropped back again to his side, 'our Mr Jones may be one hell of a sonofabitch character, whoever he is, but he's sure got the guts and spirit that brings a fella through a situation like this. There's always got to be somebody ready to stake his lot on the impossible, ain't that so?'

'It's so,' said Holden, mopping his burning face. 'But I still wouldn't offer him my back when he's really cornered. Meantime, we may just need him, Mr Deakin. Like you say, we're stakin' on the impossible and Mr Jones is a gambler, after all.'

Charlie glanced quickly at the man. 'Still can't place him, though. Can you?'

'No and there's a hell of a sight more to concentrate on right now than rummagin' round memories.' Holden narrowed his gaze on the deepening greyness ahead. 'We goin' to make that gulch?' he asked.

'In less than an hour if Mrs Pierce

keeps movin', but she ain't short of support up there. Buthnott's givin' her a hand in all the right places!'

They walked on in silence until Holden asked, 'Do you know where this water is once we reach the gulch?'

'I know precisely where it *was* two summers back when Moose and me brought a wagonload of coach spares through from Hurley Rocks to Harper's Town and discovered water at the bottom of the ravine,' said Charlie.

'Two summers back?' frowned Holden. 'But that's — '

'Two years ago, I know,' shrugged Charlie. 'But it's all we've got, ain't it? So I guess we're no better than Jones stakin' big on the impossible.'

# 8

The light had faded to the soft glow of dusk when they reached the outlying rocks flanking the gulch and, with Charlie now leading, made their way to its narrowest end.

'There's a long slope from here on,' he warned the others as they approached the point he had chosen as the safest entry on the treacherous descent to the floor of the natural ravine. 'It's a slow drop, and you can't see or tell what's comin' up next, so go easy, no rush. Once down we'll head for a place I found that's sheltered from the sun and heat and holds the water.'

You hope, thought Holden.

'Stay in line and keep to my path,' ordered Charlie. He turned to Madelaine Pierce. 'Be right behind me, ma'am, and if you feel yourself fallin' just yell out. I'll be there.'

'Same goes for me, Mrs Pierce,' grinned Buthnott. 'I'm right here.'

The woman nodded, but said nothing as she brushed at her lank, damp hair and made some attempt to pat the sand from her dress.

Holden watched and waited quietly.

Jones sighed, swallowed on his parched throat and ran his tongue over cracked, blistering lips. 'Let's move, Mr Deakin,' he croaked. 'Night's comin' in fast.'

'You got it,' answered Charlie, and turned to the slope.

★ ★ ★

Their progress over the first yards was swift and relatively easy. Footholds held firm, coverings of blown sand hid few hazards, no more than handfuls of loose rocks fell ahead of them. And what little there remained of the light held good for as long as it took them to pause halfway to the as yet unseen floor of the ravine.

'We're doin' fine, just fine,' said Charlie, easing his hat from his sticky head. 'Just keep it up and don't get to rushin'.'

'How come you ever found this place?' asked Buthnott. 'T'ain't exactly on the main trail, is it?'

Charlie cleared his throat and answered carefully. 'Well, it came about by chance, really,' he said. 'Moose and me, we were headin' out of Hurley Rocks, needed water and figured we'd take a look here. Simple as that.' He purposefully avoided catching Holden's eye.

'But you didn't bring horses down here, surely?' said Buthnott.

'No, no, we canteen'd up, filled a small barrel, hauled it all the way back to the trail . . . We got through.'

'And when did all this happen, Mr Deakin?' asked the woman.

This time Charlie could not avoid the despairing roll of Holden's eyes.

'Oh, don't rightly recall exactly when, ma'am, but it ain't that long back,' lied

Charlie, settling his hat again. 'Let's move on, shall we?'

* * *

Charlie Deakin admitted freely he was no Bible-thumper, but he had been raised proper to give thanks at the supper table and to show due regard to women, children, the sick, infirm and elderly, though he was not much for praying.

But tonight he was praying.

He was praying that Moose and he had not been dreaming or mistaken the day they had discovered the gulch pool, that it had been real, that it had always been there, a natural phenomenon and, most of all, that it was still there this very night.

It had better be, he thought, as he led the party deeper into the gulch, feeling his way like a slithering snake, the sweat cold as ice on his neck and back, throat dry as dirt, limbs heavy as stone. No water, and that would be it. The gulch would be their graveyard. They would be bones inside a month.

On the other hand, if the pool was natural, if it was there, just like he and Moose had found it — if his prayers were answered — they would live. Quite what for, to what end in this godforsaken country, he had no idea, but that was of no count right now. There was no way he was going to allow Willard Pierce the satisfaction of living in comfort all for the sake of a drop of water. But that depended . . .

It was not until Charlie felt a bed of firmer rock beneath his feet that he knew they had arrived.

He sniffed the cooler, thinner air. Moose had always reckoned you could smell water after two days in the desert. 'If it's there, it'll tell you,' he had said, tapping the side of his nose as if it were some ancient secret. Charlie sniffed again, indicated for the party to stop and wait.

'Anythin', Mr Deakin?' hissed Buthnott.

'Are we supposed to smell somethin'?' quipped Jones impatiently. 'Mebbe we should get to lookin'.'

'If it's here, I'll know it,' said Charlie, ahead of another longer, deeper sniff.

'Since when have we been expected to smell water, 'ceptin' when it's stagnant?' Jones squatted, his eyes white and staring in the thickening darkness.

Charlie said nothing as he indicated for them to follow him to the left. His steps were slow, easy, one ahead of the other but only when he reckoned it safe to move on. He was conscious of Madelaine Pierce stumbling, of Buthnott's hand in support, the murmured thanks, the shuffle of feet.

He had been reaching blindly into a darkness that seemed to envelop them now like a cloak, when he stopped, sniffed again and knew without a doubt that he had found it. The pool of clear water was here, exactly where he had found it the last time. Right under his nose.

★ ★ ★

'We got lucky, but we're goin' to need a whole heap more come sun-up.' Jones trickled a handful of sand to the rocks between his feet, then settled back on his elbows and stretched his legs. 'Agreed, Mr Holden?'

Charlie, Jones and Holden were seated in a tight group some distance from the pool behind a shelving of boulders. A reach of the pale moonlight lit their faces as if holding a soft flame to them. They could hear the slow movement of water, the occasional splash as Madelaine Pierce bathed in privacy at the pool. Buthnott, his mind half on the group, half on his personal images of the woman, sat aside in shadow. They had all sated their thirsts, doused their heads in water until they seemed to wash away the searing heat of the day.

Charlie could cheerfully have fallen into a deep sleep, but to do so down here in his current situation might prove fatal. And he still had his responsibility

77

to the well-being and safety of his passengers, in spite of the assumed leadership of the unknown Mr Jones. Or perhaps it was because of him.

Holden weighed a small stone thoughtfully in his right hand, ran the fingers of his left over its smooth, cool surface, then tossed it ahead of him into the darkness. 'It's sun-up that bothers me,' he said quietly. 'What are our chances, Mr Deakin?'

Charlie blinked out of a threatening doze. 'Well, one thing's for dead-sure certain, we can't take this water with us, and we've some sonofabitch hot distance to go yet to the hills. Best we can do is soak everythin' we can — bandannas, cloths, rags, anythin' — and keep 'em damp for as long as possible. I'd reckon on us makin' that climb out of here just as soon as we've enough light to see by. Don't want to be strugglin' clear in the full heat. We're goin' to need all the strength we can muster for the walk to the hills.' He glanced reluctantly at Jones. 'Like you say, a whole heap more of luck.'

Jones grunted. 'And there's somethin' else 'sides water to ponder on. Somethin' that might be a whole sight more troublesome.'

Charlie frowned. 'And what's that?'

'Willard Pierce has just pulled off one of the biggest heists this territory's ever likely to see. Now I ain't got the damnedest notion as to how much he's scooped out of his so-called ailin' bank, but you can bet your sweet life it's one helluva haul. He wouldn't have gone to the trouble he has for a cent less than a fortune, and he's still got the likes of Coe and his henchmen to pay off.' Jones's gaze darkened on the faces turned to him. 'But he's made one mistake,' he added slowly.

'Us,' said Holden. 'We're his mistake. He's left us to die when he should have shot us back there at the stage.'

'Precisely, Mr Holden,' smiled Jones. 'We're the godalmighty flaw in an otherwise faultless plan. And even now, at this very minute, I'm figurin' Pierce has realized it. He's got to thinkin' that we could get lucky; could by some miracle of chance, survive and live to tell the tale of what happened out there on the regular stage service, Harper's Town to Rainwater. So then what's he goin' to do? What'll be his thinkin', Mr Deakin? What would you do in his boots?'

Charlie swallowed. 'Hell, I'd sure want to make certain we were dead. Double-check. Know for sure.' He blinked. 'Hell, I'd send a handful of the scumbags back to the desert to *make* sure. You bet I would!'

'You got it, Mr Deakin, on the nose,' said Jones, sitting upright. 'That's exactly what'll be waitin' for us when we climb out of this gulch at first light. Guns and rats under orders to shoot on sight. So without a single gun between us, how we goin' to handle them? Any suggestions?'

The only response to Jones's question was a piercing, high-pitched scream from Madelaine Pierce at the water pool.

# 9

Jones was the first to his feet, followed by Holden hard on his heels, with Charlie bringing up the rear as the three men scrambled over the rocks and through the sand, rounded the cover of boulders and stumbled, slithered towards the pool.

Charlie felt a sickening knot of chill in his stomach at the sight of the woman's clothes scattered across the sand. 'What in the name of all hell . . .' he muttered as the three came to the rippling surface of the pool and could see, clear in the shafted moonlight, the naked figure of the woman standing some few feet from the edge, the water lapping gently at her knees, her eyes wide and staring, hair long and loose across her back and shoulders, her whole body locked in spasms of violent shuddering.

Jones swung round to where Buthnott was crawling on hands and knees through the sand, away from the pool, his pants heavy with water, his shirt sodden.

'Get the woman out of there and into some clothes, f'Chris'sake,' ordered Jones, already heading into the chase to reach Buthnott before he disappeared into the darkness.

Holden waded into the pool and lifted Madelaine Pierce in his arms. Charlie scooped up her clothes and together they settled the shivering woman on the softer sand in the lee of the boulders.

'Ain't no point to askin' what happened here, ma'am, I reckon we can all guess,' said Charlie, swallowing on a tight, pinched throat as he turned to locate Jones and Buthnott.

'Get dried and dressed best you can, ma'am,' said Holden quietly. He wiped sweat and dirt from his face then crossed to Charlie's side. 'Where's Buthnott?'

'Can't you hear?' murmured Charlie, easing a few more steps from the boulders. 'Gettin' the hidin' of his life from a man I'd rate for bein' pretty deadly at handin' out hidin's.'

'Mebbe,' said Holden, narrowing his gaze in the general direction of the sounds of the beating being meted out. 'But if we let him, Jones'll kill the fella.'

'Perhaps that's no bad thing in the circumstances,' quipped Charlie, regretting his words almost immediately. 'No,' he snapped. 'I didn't mean that. Hell, we're tiptoein' round our own graves as it is. Ain't no need to go pushin' one another into 'em.'

Holden slapped Charlie across the shoulders, glanced back at the woman hidden in the shadows of the boulders, and headed into the darkness. 'Follow me, Mr Deakin.'

★ ★ ★

It was a long, dark hour before Madelaine Pierce was fully dressed and recovered enough to sit apart but within sight of Jones, Holden and Charlie and beyond any threat from Lemuel Buthnott. Not, thought Charlie, that the storekeeper was in any fit state now to do more than tend his cuts and deepening bruises and try to mend whatever remained of his broken pride and standing.

'That's all we need,' scowled Jones, his quick glance at the man burning with contempt. 'A woman-crazed shopkeeper with about as much regard for . . . What the hell, I should've killed him.'

'You would've done if me and Holden hadn't stopped you,' said Charlie, aware of that same knot of chill in his stomach. 'But whatever he tried back there with Mrs Pierce don't alter the truth none of what Mr Holden here reckons: we're goin' to need Buthnott when we come to climbin' out of here and facin' the scum that might well be waitin' on us. And, let me remind you, we're gettin' awful close to that time.

Little short of another hour and there'll be enough light to make a start.' He gazed along the high rim of the ravine. 'Might be an idea if we left Buthnott to his demons and got to figurin' them waitin' on us.'

Jones grunted. 'Let's get to soakin' the bandannas like you said, Mr Deakin. Then we climb.'

★ ★ ★

They were on the move again in under the hour, with Jones leading, Frank Holden assisting Madelaine Pierce, followed by Charlie and finally Buthnott. The storekeeper had needed no directing to his place in the line; fact of it was, Charlie had thought, that he might well have chosen to bury himself and his shame right there in the ravine.

But Jones had not minced his words as the party prepared to move out: 'What you attempted back there, mister, was little short of rape. For that I would have shot you, and gladly, 'ceptin' I don't have a gun. But that don't alter my verdict, and I guess I mebbe speak for the others on that count too. Meantime, we need you to help get us out of this hole and face whatever we've figured might be waitin' on us. So you get a reprieve for now. But you do exactly as you're told, and not a foot wrong. You hear me?'

Buthnott had presented a pathetic figure in those final moments before the climb began, with his face swollen, cut and bruised, his lips slanted to one corner of his mouth, clothes bloody and caked with dirt and his body creased to a toad-like squat. He had said nothing, but his glance at the woman had told Charlie all he needed to know. What they had found at the pool side had all the marks of a predetermined attack on Madelaine Pierce, but was it as clear-cut as that? Heck, Charlie had thought, did it matter when their very survival was on a knife-edge?

They made fast, easy progress in the first half-hour while the air was still cool and before the light had broken fully. Jones set an eager pace, anxious to be clear of the gulch and into whatever rock cover they could find as soon as possible. It would be up to Charlie to plot their course across the desert to the hills, assuming they got the chance.

Madelaine Pierce stayed close to Holden, her energy for the climb strengthening by the minute. Some woman, thought Charlie. Tough, capable, able to recover. But, then, how many times in her unknown past had she been attacked by men? Maybe she had a whole sight more about her than at first appeared. The foremost lady of Harper's Town she might well have become, but before then, wherever it was Willard Pierce had first found her, that might be another story . . .

'Almost there, Mr Deakin,' hissed Jones through the breaking light a half-hour later. 'We'll make straight for the rocks. Rest up there 'til we see what's doin'.'

In little more than twenty minutes

they were scurrying across the sand clear of the ravine and heading for the shadows and safety of the outcrop like a line of scorpions.

* ★ ★

'Best not make a move 'til the light's full,' murmured Charlie at Jones's side where they sprawled flat across the rocks watching for the first hint of the horizon. 'If there is anybody out there we ain't for announcin' ourselves.'

Jones grunted. 'If there is anybody out there, Mr Deakin, I'd reckon for them havin' seen us already. But, like you say, we'll wait. Keep our eyes skinned and miss nothin'. You hear that, Buthnott? Keep your eyes on the dirt out there and nowhere else.'

The storekeeper squirmed, but settled a suddenly tighter, fiercer gaze on Jones, and for the first time since the beating broke his silence, his cut lips working to steady the words. 'I'm not for takin' a deal more from you, Jones — if that's who you truly are,' he slurred, a trickle of blood at the corner of his mouth. 'You're only surmisin' what happened back there. You ain't heard nothin' of my side of it.'

'No,' quipped Jones, 'and I ain't much for listenin' to you, mister. I seen, along of Mr Deakin and Holden here, what I seen. And I sure as hell saw Mrs Pierce. I ain't for needin' no schoolin' to add them together and get where I am. Now if you've got — '

'T'ain't how it seems,' levelled Buthnott, his eyes gleaming, his broken lips twitching. 'I know that woman there a whole sight better than you, Jones. Damn it, she was practically my next door neighbour, f'Chris'sake, and I could tell you first-hand stories about her goin's on behind Willard Pierce's back as would make even your hair curl! If you don't believe me, ask her. She's right here. Ask her about them afternoons she spent out back of the bank with Kent Cooper; ask her about them nights in Marty Gold's woodshed

89

when half the town men would be darn near standin' in line waitin' on — '

'All right, Lem,' snapped Charlie, 'that's enough. This ain't the place and it's sure as hell not the time.'

'Too right it ain't,' said Holden, slipping clear of his higher vantage in the rocks. 'We've got company, and it's headin' this way. Fast!'

# 10

'I got two,' murmured Charlie, squinting into the early morning gloom, 'and I figure that for bein' the lot. Two riders headin' this way from the north.'

'Me too,' confirmed Holden, a distance to Charlie's left. 'Fast pace. Been ridin' some time I'd reckon.'

Jones eased himself to clear the ridge of the rock cover. 'You recognize 'em? They Pierce's men?'

'Too far away,' said Holden, 'but I'd guess to it. Seem to know where they're goin'.'

Jones grunted and tightened his gaze on the approaching shapes. 'Question is, gentlemen, how we goin' to take 'em?'

'We're goin' to even try?' frowned Charlie.

'No choice,' said Jones. 'We need whatever water they're carryin'; we need their horses; and, not least, we need their guns.'

Charlie swallowed on that familiar icy knot in his guts and glanced quickly at Jones. Guns in that man's hands right now might not be such a good idea. 'T'ain't goin' to be easy,' he muttered.

'Impossible,' slurred Buthnott, dabbing a bandanna at his lips. 'They'll shoot us like rats in a barrel.'

Jones fumed quietly for a moment. 'If you ain't got anythin' useful to say, storekeeper, then button it, will you?' The man ran a hand across his stubbled chin where the sweat was already beginning to glisten like rain. 'There is a way, the *only* way and we're goin' to have to take it, like it or not.' He turned his dark gaze on Madelaine Pierce. 'You're our ace card, lady, and we're about to play you.'

★ ★ ★

'You can't do it,' spluttered Buthnott through a trickle of blood at his mouth.

'It ain't decent. T'ain't human.'

Jones pushed the man aside and slid across the sand and stones to Madelaine Pierce. 'Well, ma'am, what do you reckon? Will you give it a try? You're all we've got.'

The woman pulled nervously at her torn dress, flicked her hair into her neck and glanced quickly over the faces of the others watching her. Charlie Deakin looked as anxious as ever. Frank Holden his familiar enigmatic self; uncommitted, seemingly unconcerned, but probably deeply troubled about something. Or maybe someone. Buthnott was confused, bewildered; a little man caught up in a whirlwind.

'It's awful risky,' murmured Charlie.

'It's outrageous,' spluttered Buthnott again, wiping the blood from his lips. 'It's as good as puttin' Mrs Pierce out like a piece of bait. Now I may not go along with her morals, and there maybe a whole heap of indecencies and — '

'Oh, shut up, will you!' flared the

woman, her cheeks glistening, lips quivering. 'All right, so I may not be your idea or anyone else's of a paragon of virtue, but I didn't see you missin' out on a chance at the woodshed! You bet I didn't.' She swung round to face Jones. 'I'll do it. 'Course I'll damn well do it. Gladly. What do you want?'

'You've got just five minutes, murmured Holden, his gaze tight on the horizon. 'Five minutes . . . '

★   ★   ★

The riders gritted their teeth against the flying dirt and veered their mounts on a course directly for the outcrop.

'That the place we're lookin' for?' called the younger of the two above the jangle of tack, creaking leather and pounding hoofs.

'Coe reckons so,' said his partner, narrowing his gaze to slits. 'Says as how it's the only place where there's shade. He's right!'

'What if they ain't there?'

'We'll scout around for a while, then pull out. I ain't for bakin' to death in this heat.' He urged his mount to a faster pace. 'Let's just do it, eh? Get it over with, then get back in time for the big share-out. Don't want to miss out on that, eh, Franky?'

'You bet. I hear as how old man Pierce can be real generous when he's a mind.'

'You mean when his back's to the wall! Yeah, I hear so. Me, I'd have settled for him handin' me that wife of his. Now there, my friend, was some woman . . . '

The younger rider pointed ahead to the dark bulks of the outcrop. 'Eh, Marty, you see that? There's somebody there. Dead ahead. In them rocks. It's . . . Darn me if that ain't the woman. That's Mrs Pierce!'

'Sonofabitch, I do believe you're right, Franky. Well, now, if that ain't some mirage fit to gladden a man's heart.'

'She ain't no mirage, Marty. She's

real enough. She's alive. She's survived, goddamnit. Ain't this our lucky day. And don't you go tellin' me you're goin' to shoot her, 'cus I ain't for hearin' it. Right? But, hell, what are we goin' to do? We're under orders, Marty. Shoot anyone still alive. No survivors. Them's Pierce's very words.'

'I know. I heard 'em clear enough. Hell . . . '

The riders came on at a whipping, dust-swirling pace, the already hot air scorching their faces, burning into their eyes as they took in the sight of Madelaine Pierce standing at the base of the rocks her bare legs and feet straddling the sand, her dress torn, eyes wide and wild, hair bedraggled at her shoulders, the sweat gleaming like a scattering of diamonds across her exposed flesh.

They reined back and halted in a final swirl of dust and simply sat and stared in silence.

★　★　★

The man called Marty wiped the dirt and sweat from his face. 'You all right, ma'am?' he asked, his voice as thick as gravel.

The woman opened her eyes as if waking from a trance. 'What do you think?' she croaked.

'Didn't expect to find nobody alive,' said Franky, blinking the dirt from his eyes.

'I bet you didn't!' scoffed the woman. 'So why are you here? To kill off any twitching remains? Were those my husband's orders?'

A nerve jumped in the younger man's cheek. Marty leaned forward in his saddle. 'Mite lippy there for somebody in your predicament, ain't you, lady?' he said, a soft, lascivious grin at his dried lips. 'Where's the others?' he added bluntly, his gaze reaching beyond the woman to the rocks behind her.

'All dead. All gone.' Madelaine Pierce gestured an arm loosely over the desert. 'I don't know where. Can't recall.'

Marty's stare narrowed. 'So how come you're alive? You got some special powers or somethin'?'

The woman shrugged. 'Can't say,' she quipped, looking away. 'One of those things, I suppose. I just got lucky.'

Marty spat fiercely into the dirt. 'Best take a closer look, Franky,' he grunted. 'We want to see bodies.'

'What about me?' said the woman anxiously. 'You aren't going to leave me here, are you? Not now. I mean, I always figured there might be somebody ride out to check on us. That would be typical of Willard. Check and check again, like he was reckoning a column of figures. He doesn't change. But now that you boys are here . . . ' She flicked her hair provocatively. 'Well, what are you going to do?'

Franky licked his lips. 'I'll go take a closer look like you say, Marty.' He dismounted, drew his Colt from its holster and passed slowly into the outcrop, his steps measured and careful.

Madelaine Pierce smiled. 'He won't find anything. There's nothing there.' She swallowed and ran the back of her hand across her mouth. 'Wouldn't happen to have some water handy, would you?'

'It's goin' to cost you,' grinned Marty, reaching for his canteen. 'Water don't come cheap out here, 'specially when it's you askin'.'

'I'm sure you're right, but you needn't worry. I'll pay the price in full. I always do.' She took the canteen and put it to her lips.

Marty watched her for a moment then frowned, began to sweat and levelled his gaze on the shape emerging beyond her. 'Franky?' he murmured hoarsely. 'Franky . . . That you there? What in the name of hell . . . ?'

'Your partner just got his head stoved in with a rock, my friend,' hissed Jones, as he let the Colt in his grip blaze freely across the thick morning air. 'And, like you see, I've borrowed his shooter for a while.'

He smiled cynically. 'Good day, Marty!'

The gun blazed again and Marty slid from his mount as if he had melted in the heat.

# 11

Four pairs of eyes were fixed on Jones like lights. Four faces watched in silence. Nobody moved. It seemed as if they all might have stopped breathing. Finally, Madelaine Pierce stretched her arms across her breasts to hug herself against a sudden shiver in spite of the thickening heat of the day. She stared at the man for a moment and murmured, 'He's dead.'

'Both of 'em dead, lady,' grinned Jones, securing the Colt to his belt. 'That's two less to bother us and meantime we help ourselves to horses, water and guns. Not a bad start to the day, eh?'

Still nobody spoke; still they simply stared from Jones to the body and back again.

'Well, don't all get to thankin' me in such a hurry, will you?' quipped Jones, shoving his hat clear of his brow. 'I mean, what do you want? You expectin' me to bury these sonsofbitches all decent and reverent? You want me to say words over 'em? Hell, they were here to finish us off, and would've done too if the lady here hadn't shown some real guts in standin' to 'em and if I — '

'I think we're all aware of what you did, Mr Jones,' said Charlie. 'And I guess we are indebted to you and to Mrs Pierce, but it's mebbe that we ain't so used to killin' as — '

'As what?' snapped Jones. 'Why don't you say it — as I am? Ain't that what you're thinkin'?'

'You did it awful easy on both counts,' said Buthnott. 'Back there with the rock that killed the fella, and here with the gun.'

'Sure I did,' flared Jones. 'You know why? They call it survival of the sharpest, the fastest, the one with the edge. That's why we're all still standin' here and breathin', and that's why in only a matter of minutes we're goin' to be headin' clear across that goddamn sand to them hills where we might, we just might, stand a chance of comin' out of this almighty mess in somethin' like one piece.'

★ ★ ★

They moved out from the outcrop into the scorching morning, Madelaine Pierce mounted on one of the two mounts taken from the gunslingers. 'We'll share the other between us,' Jones had announced, already slipping a foot to the stirrup. 'One hour each, then we change.'

'What about the weapons?' Holden had asked, his eyes narrowing carefully on the collection gathered on the sand.

Jones tapped the Colt in his belt. 'I'll keep this,' he said. 'There's another Colt, two rifles, couple of knives. Sort 'em as you think. We've got water and rope — what more do we need, savin' mebbe a lifetime's supply of luck? But a man can't get picky out here. Let's go.'

They trailed slowly towards the shimmer of the distant hills, their steps as scuffed and lifeless as the mount's reluctant response to Jones's urgings.

'Do you think we'll make it, Mr Deakin?' Buthnott wheezed a few steps behind Charlie and Holden. 'It sure as hell looks a long way to them hills.' He shielded his eyes against the glare as he scanned the horizon.

'Take it from me, it is,' said Charlie, wincing at the bite of sand between his toes. 'One sonofabitch mile piled on more sonofabitch miles. And there ain't no easy way.'

Buthnott wiped the sweat from his face. 'But at least we have water,' he croaked.

Charlie winced again, halted, removed the boot from his right foot and released a stream of gritty dirt back to the sand. 'We have water for just as long as we go easy with it. When them murderin' rough-necks canteens are empty, that's it for an awful long way through an awful long time.'

Buthnott gulped as if swallowing for the last time, and trudged on in silence.

Charlie eased his steps towards Holden. 'I still ain't for trustin' Jones,' he murmured, wondering now if he should come clean about what he had been told by Thake Todd. 'I just get the feelin' he might take it into his head to pull clear of the rest of us anytime he fancies, 'specially now we're free of Pierce's men and he's armed.'

'Not a deal we can do to stop him, Mr Deakin,' grunted Holden, 'save shoot him in the back, o'course.' He grinned. 'Mebbe not, eh? Wouldn't serve no purpose.' His gaze went back to the distant blue-grey blur of the hills. 'More pressin' is how long before our friend Mr Willard Pierce gets suspicious about the absence of the men he sent out to clear up any loose ends. He ain't exactly the type to leave matters to chance.' He grunted again. 'How long before he sends out more men? Or suppose he gets Coe to leave somebody waitin' in the hills . . .'

'Hold it,' said Charlie, laying a hand on Holden's arm. 'There's somethin' out there. I'm darn sure I saw — '

'Easy now,' called Jones, reining his mount to a halt. 'Is that what I think it is, Mr Deakin?' he asked, pointing ahead to a thickening cloud of dust drifting like a ghost towards them. 'Is that riders?'

'You got it,' said Charlie. 'Them's riders, and comin' at a lick.'

'Pierce's men?' croaked Buthnott.

'Hold your ground here,' snapped Jones, wheeling his mount through a tight circle. 'I'll try to draw them off. I suggest you dismount, lady, and stay with the others.' He urged his horse into action. 'I'll be back, don't you fret,' he yelled, as the mount surged ahead heading due west on a slack rein.

'Hell, I might have known!' Charlie flung his hat to the ground and spat. 'Just like I was figurin', first chance he gets and he's away, faster than a fly to dung. Sonofabitch! Why, for two pins I'd shoot him in the back myself.'

'Don't waste the effort,' said Holden,

above what had now become the pound of beating hoofs. 'Let's concentrate on the company we've got ridin' in.'

★ ★ ★

'Hold tight to that horse, lady,' murmured Holden, wiping his eyes and then shielding them against the fierce glare as he watched the riders growing ever closer. He swallowed. 'How many? Any idea?'

'Sounds like dozens of em,' said Buthnott, the sweat beading angrily on his face.

'Have they been sent by my husband?' asked the woman. She drew the mount to her and stroked its nose.

'That I very much doubt, ma'am,' said Charlie. 'They're comin' from the wrong direction. That bunch, whoever they are, are comin' from the east — and the east is the last place your husband would want to be right now. Too many folk. No, these are somethin' else.'

'But who?' sweated Buthnott, fumbling

uselessly with his sodden bandanna. 'Can't we do somethin'?'

Holden shifted the range of his gaze to focus on the fast disappearing dust cloud of Jones. 'So much for our friend's scheme,' he muttered almost to himself. 'It ain't workin'. Jones is ridin' clear, but nobody's followin'.'

'Just like the sonofabitch figured, I'll bet,' growled Charlie, spitting again. 'But if he thinks he's gettin' away, he can think again. I tell you somethin', when I get back to — '

'Easy,' urged Holden, calming Charlie's anger. 'It's too late now to worry about Jones. We'll get to him mebbe. That is, we will if we manage . . . '

The leading riders of the bunch slithered their mounts to a jangling halt and waited for the dust to settle.

★ ★ ★

At first they could see only eyes; round, gleaming eyes that devoured and did not blink.

Madelaine Pierce shuddered and clung to the rein of the mount as if clutching a lifeline. Buthnott broke into another bout of sweating, his face seeming to balloon to near bursting point. Holden stood easy, almost casual, one leg taking the weight of his body without a strain. A Colt nestled in his belt, a rifle unassuming in his left hand.

Charlie stared, his gaze narrowing as he struggled to see through the grey dusty gloom to make out the faces of the riders, now looking to be no less than a dozen in number. 'You fellas passin' through?' he croaked, his voice cracking on a brittle dryness. ' 'Cus if you are, we're sure as Christmas one helluva deal pleased to see you, seein' as how we've been robbed and left for dead in this godforsaken country by a bunch of no-good . . . '

His voice faded as if smothered in a sudden sand-storm. A mount was urged a few steps forward by a taller, deeply tanned rider with a slanting jaw and a dribble of bright saliva in the corner of his mouth. 'Who is the one who rode out?' he asked in a voice that seemed to gurgle like water over rocks and thicken the dribble to a stream.

'Oh, him,' grinned Charlie, shrugging. 'That was Mr Jones. He's one of us, which is to say he *was* one of us 'til just now when he took it into that loose head of his to pull clear. Kinda panicked, I guess. But he ain't no threat.'

'He will not get far,' said the man. 'I have others waiting.' He waved a rider to his side. 'Search them. Take their weapons. Take care of the woman, Sangro. No handling her, you understand. Not yet. You can have her later.'

'Now, just you look here,' said Buthnott, raising an arm. 'The lady is — '

The crack and lash of a whip in Sangro's grip wheeled across Buthnott's back like a lick of flame.

'Rope them,' ordered the man with the dribble. 'Let's move!'

# 12

They stumbled, slithered, fell, regained their feet; were dragged on mercilessly at the end of rope lines bound at their wrists as the riders set their horses to a steady pace and headed for the foothills of the distant mountain range.

'Another half-mile and I'll be down for keeps,' gasped Charlie, swinging crazily on a suddenly tautened rope. 'Can't keep this up.'

'Who are they? Any ideas?' called Holden as Buthnott's body slithered to the sand like a beached whale.

'Drifters. Chancers. No-gooders who scrounge out what they want where they find it,' groaned Charlie through a long creasing wince. 'Just our luck, eh? They'll sell Mrs Pierce on in the next town if she survives that far.' He spun for a moment like a top, found his balance again and stumbled on. 'Tell you one thing, it's doubtful if they've crossed Pierce or Coe's men. Might be an edge for us.'

'Do a deal?' spluttered Holden, spitting hot sand.

'Might be worth a try. These scum'll follow money like ants to apple pie.'

Buthnott groaned, moaned, his body rolling lifelessly. Sand skimmed at his sides to a wake at his heels like waves across a broken surface.

'For God's sake, hold up there, will you?' shouted Holden, his voice cracking and pitching almost to a scream.

Madelaine Pierce, her mount led by the sidekick, Sangro, joined the appeal. 'Please . . . please. A man is dying here. Please wait.'

The horses came to a halt. Faces, tanned, grubby, unshaven, unremitting, turned to face the three roped captives, but no one dared to speak until the man with wet lips and a dribble at the corner of his mouth reined his mount to Holden.

'This fella can't go on,' said Charlie,

nodding to the unmoving bulk of Buthnott, face-down in the sand. 'Not unless you want to kill him right here, right now.'

'Who are you, anyway?' spluttered Holden through teeth crusted with sticky dirt.

The man stared for a moment. He tightened his grip on the reins, then sighed, grunted, spat. 'You will call me Reece. Just that.' He gestured to one of his men. 'Go fetch Luke. Have him bring the wagon up. Shift!' He turned to Holden again, glanced quickly at the woman then at Charlie. 'Get him on his feet,' he ordered. 'He ain't no use dead.' His shoulders twitched. Trickles of sweat disappeared into his neck to stain his shirt instantly. 'We'll wait,' said the man. 'Meantime, who are you? Who is the one who rode out? And why only two horses between you?'

'Ah,' said Charlie, ducking clear of a pestering fly, 'now that, mister, is one helluva tale yet to be told.'

'I'm listenin'.' said Reece, relaxing. 'Tell me.'

'Any chance . . . ' pleaded Charlie, holding up his tied wrists.

'None,' grinned Reece. 'Just talk.'

★ ★ ★

Charlie wasted neither time nor words in telling of the fate of the stage since its departure from Harper's Town, the overnight stay at Bloodrock, the subsequent hijacking of the outfit by Willard Pierce and the gunslinging sidekicks led by Coe.

'Shot my partner Moose Topper in cold blood. Sure they did. Right there before my very eyes. Scum!' Charlie spat and shook the sweat from his brow. Reece and his men watched and listened in silence. Buthnott gasped, groaned and threatened to collapse again at any moment. Holden shifted his weight from one leg to the other. Madelaine Pierce sat her mount without moving, as if in a state of trance.

Charlie continued the tale. ' 'Course, Pierce'd figured on us eatin' dirt long before midnight. What he hadn't reckoned on was us findin' water at the outcrop or leastways, me rememberin' it was there.' He spat again. 'We knew he'd send men back to check on us, but we took care of them sure enough. Which ain't strictly true seein' as how Mrs Pierce there and Jones did all the real work. Then you showed up. I tell you straight, mister, this just ain't pannin' out to be our day. On the other hand, Jones has ridden clear, ain't he?' Charlie grinned, tempted to reveal what might well be the true identity of Jones. 'What you goin' to do about him? And what — '

'To hell with Jones,' groaned Buthnott, spitting sand through already dirt-crusted lips. 'What about us? What about Mrs Pierce? Look here, Mr Reece, if it's a question of money for you and your men, well, let me tell you that I am the sole proprietor of one of the wealthiest commercial ventures in

Harper's Town — if not, indeed, the territory — and I'd be more than happy to — '

'Will somebody shut him up?' rasped Reece.

A whip cracked. Buthnott's mouth closed. Silence settled for a moment.

'You know where this man Pierce has taken the stage?' asked Reece, his stare darkening on Charlie as he lit a cheroot and blew the smoke casually into the heat.

'Wouldn't know,' said Charlie. 'But I'd make a pretty good guess. I'd figure for him headin' into the hills to get organized; dispose of the stage, plan his next move, then take as many men as he reckons necessary and head for the border. He won't waste time. He can't afford to. The stage company will be joinin' up with whatever posse is raised out of Harper's Town or Rainwater. Mebbe both. Could be up to fifty men, and mebbe, more, scourin' these deserts and hills. Time ain't on Pierce's side and for once in his life it's somethin' he can't buy. He's got to make every minute count. I'm sure Mr Holden here would agree.'

Holden merely grunted as he shielded his eyes against the glaring haze and focused on the fast-growing dust cloud moving towards them.

'That'll be Luke bringin' in the wagon,' said a sidekick joining Reece.

'Good,' said Reece. 'We'll load these men then ride for Raven Rocks. Be there by nightfall. Understood? Nightfall.'

'You got it, boss,' murmured the man.

Charlie sighed, glanced at Holden, and shrugged. 'No idea,' he muttered as if in answer to Holden's questioning frown.

★　★　★

'Where we headin'?' said Holden above the spin of wagon wheels, the creaks of timber and jangling tack on strained leather.

Charlie glanced round him at the flanking riders, at Madelaine Pierce, her mount still under Sangro's control; at Reece leading the men in a relentlessly steady line for the mountain range, and finally at Buthnott, slumped like a deflated toad on the planking seat opposite him. 'I heard talk of Raven Rocks,' he called against the noise and beating hoofs, 'but I ain't never been there. They say it's deep and kinda lost. Ideal for this bunch.' He nodded to Reece's back. 'What you make of him?'

' 'Bout the same as yourself, I reckon.'

'Says it all,' said Charlie.

They sat in silence, their knuckles whitening on their grips to hold a balance against the constantly slewing and bouncing wagon. The sweat dripped freely from their faces, spread in darkening stains across their backs, gleamed and glistened then yellowed to a gritty mass as the lathering filled with flying sand. The pace increased at a signal from Reece. The noise grew. Buthnott wiped his face. Holden continued to focus his stare on the horizon.

Charlie called again above the noise. 'Any sign of Jones?'

'Nothin',' answered Holden. 'Disappeared. God knows where.'

Buthnott stirred. 'Don't take much figurin',' he croaked, running the back of his hand across his mouth. 'He's done what his type always do. He's bolted. Vanished. Saved his own lousy skin. We won't see him again.' He sneered, then stiffened. 'What about Mrs Pierce? It's her we should be worryin' about. Damnit, it don't take much to fathom what these scum have in mind for her. We must do somethin'. Get away. Anythin'.'

'Easier said than done, Mr Buthnott, judgin' by what's comin' up.'

The three men tightened their gazes on the mass of the mountain shadows ahead as they grew and deepened like some giant slug gorging on the land.

'We're headin' into that lot, Mr Buthnott,' said Charlie. 'And from where I'm sittin' I wouldn't give a dead fly's leg for comin' out — leastways, not alive.'

# 13

It was noon, with the sun still fierce in a cloudless blue sky when they passed into night. Or so it seemed to Charlie as Reece led the wagon, his mounted sidekicks and Madelaine Pierce from the scorching desert into the throat of the mountain range.

A darkness enclosed them. Sheer walls of solid rock rose on either side like vast draped cloaks. Sandy ground gave way to shale and grit, small boulders and here and there the scattered remains of skeleton bones. Sounds echoed and charged like jostling voices, and a sudden almost icy chill licked at beaded sweat.

'Into the mouth of Hell,' shuddered Buthnott, staring wildly. 'I've never seen such a place. Where does it lead? Where in God's name are we goin'?'

'You said it, mister — Hell,' murmured

Charlie, noting the sudden shiver across Madelaine Pierce's shoulders as she tightened her grip on the reins and tossed her hair nervously.

Holden slid closer to Charlie. 'Still no ideas?' he asked.

'I ain't seen none of this before if that's what you mean. Wouldn't have had need to. You'd never get a full stage and team through here. Who'd want to, anyhow?' Charlie wiped cold sweat from his brow. 'What about you? You ever been out here? No, I reckon not — like me, wouldn't have the need. Not that I know your line of business, come to think of it. What do you do, mister? Didn't hear mention of it back in Harper's Town.'

'No cause,' said Holden flatly, his gaze concentrated on the darkness ahead.

'Mebbe not,' said Charlie, 'and it ain't none of my business, but seein' as how we're here, where we are in this godalmighty mess and facin', well, who knows — '

'You noticed somethin'?' said Holden, without shifting his gaze.

'Noticed somethin'?' frowned Charlie. 'Hell, mister, I got so much to *notice* my head's spinnin' faster than a prairie twister!' He peered ahead. 'What's to notice, anyhow?'

'I'd reckon for Jones passin' through here sometime back.'

'Jones!' frowned Charlie again. 'And how do you figure that?'

'Just as we left the desert for this gulley . . . there were tracks, a single mount. Then nothin'.'

'Don't say it's for bein' Jones. Could've been one of Reece's men passin' through earlier. Damnit, this place seems to be his lair.'

'I'd figure for Jones bein' long gone,' interrupted Buthnott. 'That's typical of his kind. Didn't like the look of him minute I set eyes on him.' The storekeeper wiped his face with a sticky hand. 'We're on our own, Mr Holden. On our own.' He went back to watching the roll of Madelaine Pierce's behind.

Charlie spat over the side of the wagon. 'That fella gets to me,' he muttered under his breath. He waited a moment. 'You serious about Jones?' he said, his gaze on Holden.

'It's a possibility. Them marks were fresh, and they disappeared this way. Mebbe Jones ain't for givin' up on Pierce and that stage.'

Charlie pondered silently, then said, 'Look, mebbe there's somethin' I should tell you. Somethin' I heard from Thake back at the station.'

'That Jones is really John Bone?' clipped Holden. 'Denver Bone? I know. I been trailin' him this past twelve months.'

'But how — ' began Charlie only to be cut short by Reece's call to rein up.

★  ★  ★

Charlie's head buzzed and whirled, the sweat lathering on his brow, soaking his shirt and pants, his eyes darting like birds from Holden to Reece and back

124

again with all else becoming a blur of faces, bodies, horses, rocks, shimmering heat, sky and sand. So just who was Holden, he wondered, his mind swimming; had it been Jones who had brought him to Harper's Town, and if so, why? And how come — ?

'Are you listenin' up there, fella?' cracked Reece's voice to break Charlie's thoughts.

'Sure . . . Sure,' said Charlie, pulling himself together as he shrugged and wiped the sweat from his face. 'Must be the heat gettin' to me.'

Reece grunted. 'This is where we split,' he announced. 'I'm interested in that stage, and I wanna know more, so myself, the stage driver here and you mister,' he nodded to Holden 'and a couple of the boys will go in search of it. The old fella reckons for this Pierce fella holin' up some place while he gets himself organized. Only one place he can do that hereabouts and that's right here in these hills. If that's what he's doin', I wanna know exactly where and how strong he really is. Then we hit him. Right?'

The men nodded and murmured. Madelaine Pierce sat her mount without moving, her gaze fixed on Reece's face where the saliva dribbled freely from the corner of his mouth. Buthnott sat like a drenched toad, taking in gulps of sticky air as if any one might be his last. Holden watched in silence. Charlie licked his lips.

'You will take the woman and that gaspin' heap there to the caves, then you will wait until one of the boys returns with my orders. Do you understand?' The men nodded and murmured again. As an after thought Reece added, 'And the woman is not to be touched. Not yet.'

'Might I remind you, Mr Reece — ' began Madelaine Pierce.

'No you may not,' snapped Reece. 'You will do precisely what you are told. Otherwise, I might change my mind and feed you to the boys. And they, lady, are a hungry bunch when it comes to women. Bear it in mind.' The wet grin slid to a lopsided smile. 'We're wastin' valuable time.' He shielded his eyes and scanned the sky. 'We move with the light. Get to it.'

★ ★ ★

Charlie's head was still buzzing when some fifteen minutes later he found himself astride a mount with Holden at his side, Reece and one of his boys up ahead and a second sidekick bringing up the rear.

Holden glanced at him and murmured, 'I hope this is goin' to work. If it don't we're dead. And I wouldn't give dust for Mrs Pierce and Buthnott.'

Charlie swallowed. 'Pierce has gotta be holed-up here some place. It's his only option, 'til the heat's off. We'll find him, you'll see.'

'Wish I had your confidence,' said Holden quietly. His gaze scanned the high peaks, shimmering hillsides and shadowed boulders. 'Are we just guessin' the direction, or does anybody have the remotest idea — ' He fell silent at the signal from Reece.

The gang leader turned to Charlie. 'There's a canyon a mile or so to the North. It's wide enough to take a stage and deep enough to stay hidden. What do you reckon?'

Charlie assumed an air of careful consideration for a moment, then spat as if confirming his decision. 'Sounds ideal to me. There water there?'

'Enough,' grunted Reece.

'Any cover?' asked Holden. 'We're only five strong. No match for the bunch Pierce has recruited.'

'There's cover, if we're careful,' said Reece. 'I don't want no heroics, and if you fellas are figurin' —'

'We ain't that mule-headed,' said Charlie. 'No point in jumpin' from fryin' pan to fire. All we want . . . Yeah, well, that's another matter, ain't it?'

'It's exactly that,' grinned Reece. 'Your fate, mister, depends on what we find at the canyon. Let's pray, for your sake, that it's fruitful.'

Reece wheeled his mount and they moved on again. Charlie waited a while, then murmured, 'What about Jones? I don't see nothin' of him.'

'Hardly likely, is it?' said Holden, his gaze flat ahead. 'Well, mebbe he ain't here. Mebbe he has high-tailed it.'

'That might depend on whether or not he recognized you back there at Harper's Town.'

'And that, Mr Deakin, is somethin' we most certainly don't know.'

'Does that mean you're — ?'

'It means Jones could be waitin' his time to shoot us both in the back, assumin' Reece don't do it for him.'

Charlie gulped and cleared the sweat from his neck. 'Hell, it's a sonofabitch prospect all ends up.'

'That, Mr Deakin, is one thing we do know.'

# 14

Madelaine Pierce steadied her balance against the roll of the wagon and dismissed Buthnott's watery stare with a flick of her hair as she turned her attention to the man guarding her.

Sangro was black-haired, swarthy to the point of being almost greasy, long-limbed and as deadly, she thought, as an angry rattler. It would take very little to spark him into using the whip furled across his knees, or draw the blade from his belt and do his worst.

But he was a man and there, as far as Madelaine Pierce was concerned, lay his weakness.

She returned his gaze with the same intensity as the look in his own deep set eyes. There was no doubting what lay in his mind. But chilling the hope was the thought of Reece and the orders he had given. Nevertheless, temptation was an unrelenting master through the man's thoughts, and if he could see a way clear, he would risk satisfying it sooner or later.

'Where are we going?' she smiled as if unaware of her predicament.

'You will see,' said Sangro.

'Much further?'

The man shrugged. 'Two, three miles, mebbe more. Before the sun is down.'

Late dusk, she reckoned, noting how the shadows had lengthened and thickened since leaving the desert. She would leave her plan until then, perhaps until full nightfall when there would be less likelihood of being spotted. Meantime, she would hold Sangro's full attention for the remainder of the journey. She adjusted her dress to Buthnott's sweaty scowl, and deepened her smile. She was good at this, and knew it. After all, it had been a long time in the honing back at Harper's Town, thanks to her husband's obsession with banking.

She stifled a shudder at the thought of the man, of what he had done and the manner of its doing to reduce her to the back of a creaking wagon, sand infested and grimy in the hands of a man like Sangro. But maybe she would come out of it yet; use the charms and assets she had and make them pay. Why not — it was the cornerstone of sound banking!

She adjusted her dress again — ostensibly against the oppressive heat — stared through Buthnott and fixed Sangro firmly in her sights.

Another hour and he would be hers for the taking.

★   ★   ★

Lemuel Buthnott sighed and mopped his brow with an already sodden bandanna. That was the trouble with women like Madelaine Pierce, he thought, they never knew when to stop. Seduction by any means was all second nature, probably first. Damn it, it was all the woman had ever known and would know till her dying day. Shame, but that was life for those unfortunate enough to be trapped in it. That said, however, there was no denying . . .

He sighed again and turned his gaze to his surroundings. Nothing to be seen there with anything like the temptation and promise of Madelaine Pierce; nothing to nurture his hopes of trying to escape before it was all too late and he lay dead in the godforsaken wilderness dirt. But he was going to have to try. Of course he was. He owed it to himself, to Mrs Pierce for the moment of madness that had engulfed him back at the creek. Not that it had been all his fault. No sir. That woman had a lot to answer for, and one day she might have to; one day when she was free and alive thanks to the efforts of Lemuel Buthnott. You bet. Yessir, you bet . . .

But in the meantime there were these murderous sidekicks to reckon with, not to mention the vile terrain and merciless heat. Even so the moment would come, and when it did he would be ready and Madelaine Pierce would be grateful to him for the rest of her born days.

Now that was an interesting prospect.

★ ★ ★

The light was fading when Sangro raised an arm and gave orders to slow the pace. They passed slowly, silently into a darker passage where the sheer rock walls rose to towering heights shutting out the sky to little more than a wink.

Madelaine Pierce shivered for the first time in days, pulled her worn clothes around her and broke her concentration on Sangro. She had taken enough of him for now. Events of the past hours were crowding in. She felt suddenly angry again over the deceit and cold-blooded robbery by her husband, by the situation in which she found herself and the prospects facing her. And right now the staring eyes of Lemuel Buthnott were not helping.

'Ride ahead,' ordered Sangro to one of the riders. 'Check out the place.' The man nodded and pulled away. 'You will stay with me where I can see you,' he grinned, turning to Madelaine Pierce.

'That will be a pleasure,' she smiled in return.

Sangro shifted his dark gaze to Buthnott. 'You will stay with the men and do exactly as ordered. One foolish move, and you are dead.'

Buthnott swallowed but seethed within himself. So you may say, he thought, and I shall do just that — until I am ready. And that will be sooner rather than later . . .

He smiled softly. He was pleased with himself; pleased at his new found confidence and resolution, so much so that he was beginning to believe he might even pull if off.

Damn it, he would!

The wagon trundled on for another half-mile between the sheer walls until, with a suddenness that made Buthnott blink, they passed into a larger, lighter area that might almost have been a valley at first sight. It was enclosed within the grip of smaller rock walls in which, at ground level, a series of caves showed signs of being lived in. A makeshift lean-to housed a forge and a smithy's array of tools; a corral held a handful of horses, and a pile of wooden crates and barrels occupied a shadowed area.

'Welcome to our humble abode!' mocked Sangro, his white teeth flashing in his swarthy face.

Madelaine Pierce stayed silent and staring, her exposed flesh beginning to creep. Buthnott's eyes darted to the left, right, up, down, back again, probing, noting every nook and cranny he thought he would need for his plan to succeed.

Ten minutes later the wagon had been halted, the team unhitched, the riders dismounted, Madelaine Pierce led away to one of the caves by Sangro, and Buthnott bundled unceremoniously into the depths of another.

No one, in that first hour as the riders sated their thirsts, tended their mounts and dusted down, took the slightest notice of him. No one spoke. As far as Sangro — already preoccupied with Madelaine Pierce — and the sidekicks of Reece's gang were concerned, Lemuel Buthnott was secure in the mountain lair and a nonentity.

But that was before nightfall.

★   ★   ★

And the full night came quickly and with a density that hid the caves, the men and horses as if enclosing them in a pit. It suited Buthnott perfectly. Now, he thought, watching from the mouth of the cave where only one reluctant sidekick stood guard, he had only to wait.

The men lit a communal fire in the centre of the clearing where coffee was brewed, bacon, beef and beans cooked and the sidekicks relaxed.

Sangro finally appeared with Madelaine Pierce at his side, much to the delight of the sidekicks who lounged transfixed in the glow of the dancing flames where with a little prodding, persuasion and taunting jeers she began to writhe her limbs through a seductive dance.

Buthnott stared along with the rest, but in his case with only half his mind on the flashing arms and legs, his ears closed to the shouts of the men, the fevered atmosphere that grew with the clapping of hands, the stamping of feet.

Slowly and silently he moved across the back of the guard, well clear of his vision in the still thickening darkness. His steps fell like breaths; his movements were measured and deliberate until, as if no more than a shadow being swallowed by the evening gloom he was clear of the cave and making for the pass that had brought them to the lair that afternoon.

He wondered in one impulsive

moment if he might steal a mount from the line-hitched horses ahead of him; thought again and dismissed the notion for now. He would remain on foot until the light, then take stock of the situation. Meantime, getting free was all that mattered.

Madelaine Pierce would have to wait, fathom her own salvation which, judging by her performance round the fire where she had already started to shed some of what passed for her clothing, she was not going to find difficult.

Damn the woman, he mouthed, as he moved on closer to the pass.

Buthnott reckoned it close to midnight when the whooping and shouting at the fire finally ended and the men lapsed into drunken stupors, heady on their cheap booze and the allure of Madelaine Pierce who had disappeared without a sound into Sangro's cave.

The guard left keeping a watch on Buthnott had long since deserted his post and joined in the fireside frenzy. Now, along with the others, he snored peacefully through a whiskey-doused sleep, blissfully unaware of what he was supposed to be doing.

Madelaine Pierce had proved her worth after all, smiled Buthnott, sliding almost casually into the pass and stumbling on through the rocks and dirt for the most distant cover he could find.

He would keep going through the night until he was exhausted. Quite how far from Sangro that would take him or where in God's name he might finish up he had not the remotest idea.

Perhaps he would die of thirst in the heat; perhaps Sangro would catch up with him, or Reece discover him skulking in the rocks. Perhaps he would be dead before noon.

Where in any case would he head? How would he defend himself? Just where in this mountain hell-hole was he going to find water? Maybe he should have thought the whole thing through a deal more closely.

But by then it was too late.

# 15

Charlie Deakin could not believe his eyes. He was seeing things. Or was he? Maybe the heat had finally got to him. Maybe he was exhausted, too tired and confused to be thinking straight and seeing things for what they truly were. Maybe all this — the raid on the stage, the robbery, Pierce, Jones, Reece, the whole darned shenanigans since leaving Harper's Town — was a nightmare from which, when somebody got to stirring him, he would wake safe in the comfort of his own bed.

But, hell, this was no nightmare, no hallucination. This was for real. What he saw out there, deep in the thickening shadows as the last of the light crept away, was fact. Harsh and brutal and bloody. But fact for all that.

'What in the name of the devil's hand happened here, f'Chris'sake?' croaked one of Reece's sidekicks as he took in the scene below him.

No one answered as they continued to stare at the abandoned stage and the bodies of Coe's men who had made the desert raid strewn around it. All dead. Every last man shot and left where he had fallen. Everyone, that is, save Willard King Pierce and his gunslinging henchman Coe.

'Murdered. In cold blood,' murmured Holden. 'Some where they waited. Some where they started to run.'

Charlie released a long, low hiss of breath, swallowed hard and wiped the cold, clinging sweat from his face.

'We're too late,' grunted Reece. 'Too damned late.' He thudded a fist across his saddle, startling his mount to a rage of snorting.

'Too late here, perhaps,' reflected Holden, his eyes narrowing. 'Pierce must still have the bulk of what he filtered over time from the bank hidden somewhere and it won't be some place over the border. No, he'd have held it closer. Somewhere where it would not arouse suspicion. Another bank maybe. Somewhere in a town.' He glanced quickly at Reece and Charlie. 'How far's the nearest town?'

'Twenty-miles or more to the south-west,' said Charlie. 'That'd be Remedy. And they've got a bank there. Last one before the border. Hell, I should've figured that.'

'No matter,' said Holden. 'That'll be where Pierce and Coe are headed. That's where he'll close the deal on the robbery and head south.'

'And with one almighty payout seein' as how there ain't nobody on the payroll anymore!' mused Reece, his wet lips slanting angrily. 'Sonofabitch!' He spat. 'He's got one helluva head start, so we'll turn south-west right now. The four of us.'

'Hold on there,' protested Charlie. 'What about Mrs Pierce and Buthnott, not to mention Jones. And what about Sangro and your boys back there.

What'll they do? Damn it, what'll happen to the woman? You can't just — '

'We don't need men. And we don't need no woman. She stays with Sangro.' Reece's wet lips slid to a slanted grin. 'He'll know what to do with the precious Mrs Pierce. You bet, eh, boys?'

The two sidekicks smiled and rolled their eyes. Charlie groaned.

Holden's grip on his reins tightened. 'Charlie here and me ain't ridin' into Remedy gun-naked. Not no way. You'll have to arm us.'

Reece shrugged. 'Sure, *when* I'm ready. I'm goin' to need you fellas if I'm goin' to get my hands on that banker's heist.' He flicked his reins. 'This place stinks. Let's leave it to the buzzards.'

As if in answer to Reece's words a swoop of black wings swept across the fading light and the frenzied cries of the feasting to come echoed among the mountain peaks.

★ ★ ★

Charlie rode the next miles in a daze of images: the abandoned stage, left like so much trash to the wind and weather until it finally rotted and was blown to the desert as dust. He had been with the line better part of his life, and that particular coach had been in his personal charge almost five years, darn near since it hit the trail. Damn it, that stage had been as good as family, same as Moose Topper. Yeah, he had reflected, Moose Topper. Hell, it seemed like a life-time since the stage had been attacked and . . .

Holden reined his mount alongside. 'Deep in thought?' he asked.

'Guess so. But this ain't no time for reflectin'. In fact, it ain't no time for anythin' save what's comin' up. Can't even get to worryin' about Mrs Pierce and Buthnott. They're goin' to have to look to themselves — not that I give either of 'em a cat-in-hell's chance of survivin'. Still . . . Meantime, there's

Remedy. How in God's name — ?'

'Leave that to me,' said Holden, his eyes darkening. 'Stay close and trust me.'

'I'd find that a whole lot easier, mister, if I knew just who it is ridin' along of me. You ain't said nothin' — '

'That's goin' to have to wait. Do as I say: stay close and trust me. If we keep up this pace we're goin' to be in Remedy before Willard Pierce and company have had time to settle their thirsts.'

Charlie's hands settled to a new grip on the reins. 'I been thinkin' among other things occupyin' my mind right now, be one helluva coincidence wouldn't it, if our missin' passenger, Denver Bone, happened to turn up in Remedy? He could easily have headed that way. You could bet for certain on him makin' for the best place to stay breathin'. And mebbe he knew of Remedy. After all, a fella of his callin' gets to movin' about a bit, don't he?'

Holden smiled softly. 'He does that,

and like you say, that would be one helluva coincidence. But they do happen, Mr Deakin. Oh, yes, they do happen.'

* * *

Buthnott stirred against the early morning cold and snuggled himself deeper into the rocks. He blinked and squinted to catch the first full light as the dawn skies to the east began to thin and clear to the blue that would follow. A hot day coming up. There was some comfort in that after a bitingly icy night in the mountains. But it would be short-lived. Just a few hours from now and the heat-haze would be shimmering and the sun back to its relentless glare.

His limbs ached from his cramped position. His throat was dry and his stomach heading for his back-bone. How long, he wondered, before it all got too much for him? How long before Sangro and his boys hunted him down? They would not deal with him so absently next time. It would be painful if not terminal.

He listened. No sounds save the distant call of a hunting hawk. Nothing from the mountain lair, however far back that might be. But what of Madelaine Pierce? How had she fared through the long night? He could guess, almost see the pictures of her ordeal before him; hear her cries, screams, as one by one Sangro's men . . .

He gulped, retched. It was too much. Damn it, if he got the chance and had the means he would personally put an end to her life. It would be the kindest thing.

Hell, he thought, under the sudden beading of a chill sweat, he had to get moving, keep going, anywhere, just so long as he kept clear of Sangro. Who knows what might turn up. Why he might even meet up with one of the posses searching for the stage. Something must be moving by now; somebody must be looking for them. A scheduled stage on a respected line run by a decent company could not be simply overlooked, forgotten, dismissed. There were people involved, real lives. Nobody walked away from that, did they?

He eased slowly, achingly from his rocky hide and slithered like a lizard into the brighter light. The heat was already thickening. Another hour and it would be stifling, the air hardly breathable. He came to his feet, brushed himself down and gazed round him. Mountains, high peaks, rocks, boulders, dirt and dust. But he needed water. And soon. Which way? Only one, straight on into the sun, away from Sangro, into the unknown . . .

He was soon stumbling down the pass, too late to notice the glint of the rifle barrel that tracked his steps like an eye.

# 16

Buthnott staggered, clawed blindly at empty space and fell flat at the first shots snapping at his heels like crabs.

He lay perfectly still, not daring to twitch so much as a finger, the sweat lathering his back, trickling from his neck, his mouth desperate to spit sand. How long before steps crunched towards him; how many minutes before a long dark shadow crept across him and he heard the click of a gun hammer? That might be the last sound he would ever hear; he might be shot where he lay and left for the circling buzzards. He tried to blink, to swallow, to forget the pain that was slowly numbing his legs; to give himself to the death that was surely approaching.

A horse snorted. There were voices at a distance, somewhere behind him, higher, but not closing, not yet.

Sangro's men. There would be no mercy this time, no taking him prisoner, dragging him back to the cave to join Madelaine Pierce to await whatever grisly end Reece decided for them. This time he would be —

'On your feet,' growled a deep, gravel voice as a shadow thickened over him.

Buthnott struggled to his feet and turned to face the band of half-dozen men watching him. No sign of Sangro, but there was no mistaking the intent in these black staring eyes. God willing they would make it quick, he thought, beginning to shiver in spite of the heat and the sweat on his back.

'Rope him,' ordered the gravel voice.

Two men dismounted instantly and had Buthnott's wrists tied within seconds. A minute later he was being dragged at the end of the rope, fighting for every foothold, every sway and roll to hold his balance, back to Sangro's lair, his mind reeling with a dozen images of the torture and abuse to come until he finally died and gave thanks for the release.

But in spite of the mayhem of his thoughts, the surging sweat, pain-numbed joints and muscles, he was surprised to realize just how much ground he had covered since breaking free the previous night. Another hour, two at the most, and he might have made it. The irony of it was that he might not have been here at all if he had left his visit to Rainwater another week, as he had planned originally. It was only the fact that he had come to hear that Madelaine Pierce would be aboard the scheduled service that week that had persuaded him to join it.

Ah, yes, he thought, groaning aloud at the pain as he stumbled and cracked his shin yet again, the infamous Madelaine Pierce. She had a lot to answer for. Indeed, she had . . .

And Lemuel Buthnott might have been prepared even now, after all that had happened, to listen to her with a sympathetic and attentive ear, to give her the benefit of the doubt and see her in a new light.

But what he was not prepared for, not in his wildest dreams, was the sight that greeted him as Sangro's men finally reached the lair and threw him to his knees in front of the man himself.

★ ★ ★

He saw boots, scuffed and worn; he saw pants, dirt-smeared and filthy, on legs straddled well apart, and he could smell Sangro, the liquor and smoke soaked clothes, even at this distance. But it was what he saw through Sangro's legs that made his eyes bulge and his throat feel like a parched sandpit.

Madelaine Pierce had changed, literally overnight, from the distressed and bewildered wife of a ruthless criminal banker, thrown aside like so much trash in her fine dresses and jewels, who by some miracle had survived the remorseless heat and deprivation of the desert wilderness, to a sleek smooth, lynx-eyed

153

bandit dressed in high, polished boots, tailored pants and clean shirt, complete with a black stiff brimmed hat that shaded her finely featured face.

Buthnott swallowed. This was not the same woman he had left only hours ago to the whims and greedy fancies of Sangro's bunch of roughnecks. It could not be. But it was. No mistaking. The woman he saw right there just yards away, was Madelaine Pierce.

'She looks good, eh?' grinned Sangro, squatting to Buthnott's level to stare him directly in the eye. 'But she surprises you. Of course. So let me explain. Mrs Pierce is now one of us, Mr Buthnott, one of Sangro's bunch. She has joined us. And why not, eh? What has she to lose? Nothing. She has nothing, save her hatred for her murderous, thieving husband on whom, Mr Buthnott, she plans to wreak the most painful revenge, and her desire shared by my good self to ensure that the stolen fortunes now in her husband's hands, are shifted by whatever means to her. And, of course, me. Good, eh? You like it?'

Buthnott swallowed again as he struggled to his feet, his whole body a mass of aches and pains wallowing in a sea of sweat. He blinked like a lost owl. 'I hardly know what to say,' he croaked. 'I mean I can't believe . . . It doesn't seem possible.' He was seized by a sudden panic. 'What about me?' he mumbled. 'Does this mean — ?'

'The lady has asked particularly that we do not kill you here and now as I had intended.' Sangro's grin broadened to a cynical smile. 'She wants to keep you. Later, when she tires of having you on a leash, she will no doubt devise some means for your disposal. Should be interesting. Meantime, we ride.'

'Where to?' flustered Buthnott, unable to take his eyes off the woman. 'I thought we were supposed to wait here until Reece returned.'

'Quite so,' said Sangro. 'But Mrs Pierce and I have been talking between other things and we both feel her husband and his gunslingers have headed for a town somewhere. Some place where this banking heist can be completed quickly. The nearest town is Remedy. So Remedy it is.'

He circled the tip of his boot through sand. 'You will understand, I and the men here cannot afford to let my good friend Reece satisfy his own greed alone. It would not be fair, would it? And then there's Mrs Pierce . . . ' He gestured widely with his arms.

'But what about Mr Deakin and Mr Holden, not to mention that Jones fella wherever he may be? And then there's — '

'We leave in an hour,' snapped Sangro, his mood suddenly darker as he stepped closer to Buthnott. 'You have no time to concern yourself with the fate of others. You are lucky to be alive. Be grateful.'

Buthnott's face erupted in another surge of sweat. Madelaine Pierce simply stared, reducing the confused store-keeper to a near blubbering wreck in a world where nothing made any sense anymore.

* * *

Miles distant from the sweltering heat in Sangro's lair on that same morning, Reece had called the first halt of the day after a steady night ride, and ordered that Charlie, Holden and the two sidekicks water their mounts at the shady creek they had reached.

'Make the most of it, horses and men. I ain't for stoppin' again 'til I can see Remedy.'

Charlie waited until he was alongside Holden at the water creek before he spoke. 'We still goin' along with this crazy caper?' he whispered.

'No choice,' said Holden. 'We make a break for it now and Reece will gun us like flies. And we ain't armed. Not yet. Best to wait 'til we reach Remedy. Reece is goin' to need us there. He won't wait for Sangro joinin' him.' He glanced quickly at the man where he stood in deep conversation with his sidekicks. 'He's got big things in his sights, and high hopes of grabbin' 'em.'

Charlie dipped his canteen into the water and watched the slow gurgle of bubbles break the surface. 'You goin' to tell me more about you and Denver Bone?' he murmured.

'Not a word,' returned Holden. 'He'll wait 'til Remedy. And that's where he'll be. You bet to it.'

'All right you two,' growled Reece, crossing towards them. 'Cut the talkin'. Get yourselves resigned to Remedy. After that ... ' He shrugged, spat across a hot rock and cleared a beading of sweat from his brow. 'Unknown. Just be grateful I ain't had the boys here leavin' you for crow meat.'

'Takin' an awful big gamble, ain't you?' said Charlie through a steady stare.

'Gamble?' frowned Reece, flicking the sweat from his fingers to the ground. 'How you seein' that, fella? Only gamble hereabouts is how long you and your partner have got to stay breathin'.'

'That's number one gamble for you,' grinned Charlie, posing an expression of confidence. 'Then there's Jones and mebbe a sheriff's posse headin' right on our tails as I speak. Not to mention Sangro. What's he goin' to reckon when you don't show back in the mountains? I'll tell you what he's goin' to figure. He's goin' — '

Reece's clenched fist crashed into Charlie's cheek like a hurled rock, throwing him to the dirt with a thud. 'No more talking,' spat Reece. 'Not if you want to see the rest of this day. Now mount up.' He gestured to his men. 'Keep a close watch on the pair of 'em. One step out of line, shoot 'em, just bad enough to leave 'em to bleed to death.'

The sidekicks grinned. Holden gritted his teeth. Charlie wiped the blood trickling from the corner of his mouth.

It was going to be a long day.

# 17

Remedy was a halfway town. Not so much in terms of where it lay, but for what it had become. Neither poor nor prosperous; handsome or ugly; memorable or easily forgotten. You could ride into Remedy and stay a lifetime without it offending, displeasing or being too easy-going and generous. Or you could ride straight through and never notice a darn thing.

It had been a halfway place for those who had arrived in town in the last few days.

Willard Pierce and his sidekick had ridden in trailing two packhorses and little else save Coe's weapons and what they stood in. They had been greeted even before they had hitched their mounts and dismounted by Julius Catch, president and sole factotum of Remedy's only but highly regarded bank where Pierce's personal accounts were held in some esteem, if only for their ever-growing amounts over the past few years.

'Welcome to Remedy, Mr Pierce, welcome indeed,' Catch had beamed, crossing the dusty, glare-lit street to meet them. 'And to what do we owe this honour?'

'Strictly business, Mr Catch, no more, no less. But business of a high order, I assure you, so let us get to work without delay.'

'By all means, Mr Pierce. The pleasure is mine. I am at your disposal. Might I suggest a private room at the Pearl Saloon rather than the formality of my office. Unless, of course — '

'The saloon will do well enough, Mr Catch. Lead on. My friend Mr Coe here will attend to the horses.'

It was within minutes of this encounter that Sheriff Frank Cottle took an interest in the new arrivals over a freshly brewed pot of coffee with Doc Parker.

'What's on your mind, Frank?' asked Doc, settling himself in the only comfortable chair in Cottle's sparsely furnished office. 'You look a might thoughtful there.'

The sheriff had strolled quietly to the window overlooking the street before answering. 'I'm just wonderin',' he began, rubbing the dark stubble on his chin. 'How come a man like Willard Pierce is keepin' the company of the types of Coe.'

'You know Coe?' said Doc, sampling his coffee.

'Of him. Just a two-bit fella out for a fast dollar wherever he can pick it up. Had an unsavoury bunch ridin' along of him at one time. Seems to have deserted 'em for some reason.' He folded his arms dramatically. 'And what's Pierce doin' ridin' in like a man who's been desert-whipped for days? Why ain't he arrivin' in style? I hear he usually does.'

Doc tapped a finger on the arm of the chair. 'Man with money can do most things he has a fancy for.'

Cottle unfolded his arms and turned his back on the window. His stare was steady and levelled. 'Pack horses is pushin' it some, ain't it?'

Doc Parker offered no comment.

★ ★ ★

By noon on that day Remedy had received another visitor, but without any of the warmth of recognition and welcome afforded to Willard Pierce.

John Denver Bone arrived without a whisper of greeting. The man simply hitched his tired looking mount at the town's communal water trough, gazed round him with the careful eye of one who rated knowing where to hide well ahead of where to eat and sleep, dusted himself down and headed for the Pearl Saloon without so much as a cent in his dirt-gritty pockets.

He threaded his way through the crowded bar, gestured to the barman and spoke quietly. 'You got a fella name of Pierce stayin' here? Willard Pierce. Banker out of Harper's Town.'

'Sure,' said the barman, sweeping a cloth across the wet bar. 'Back room right now. Private meetin'.'

'Well, now, you just get a message to Mr Pierce from me, eh? You go tell him as how Mr Jones is in town, right here in the bar.'

The barman swept the cloth through a wider sweep. 'Do what I can when I got the time. Pretty busy right now.'

Jones grabbed the barman's open-neck shirt and pulled him to within inches of his grubby face. 'I want you to go now, mister. And that means just what it says in the way I'm sayin' it. *Now.*'

He released the barman who stood back, stared for a moment, thought better of any reaction and slid away to the private room at the far end of the bar. He tapped tentatively on the door and pressed himself closer for a response. Seconds later the door had opened and the man disappeared.

Jones leaned on the bar, a soft smile at his lips.

★ ★ ★

It was within an hour of Jones's arrival in Remedy that Sheriff Cottle summoned the eyes and ears of the town to his office.

Squinty Poult had never had a job or done a day's work in his life. He had never had the need to. He had been born a scavenger. Some said it was in the blood; others that it was a preferred, even cultivated, lifestyle. Whatever, Squinty had it. But with a difference.

He had figured early on that scavenging for purely material gain had its limits — you could only 'own' so much of anything at any given time. Real riches lay in dealing information: gossip, talk; what could be seen, heard, and then — for the real prize — communicated, passed on, sold. And at a price.

Squinty had quickly proved a master

in his chosen profession. So much so, that even the law had succumbed to his often deeper knowledge. Sheriff Cottle had offered to make him an official deputy, but Squinty had declined the offer on the grounds that it would — put delicately — 'compromise' his position. Squinty always had only his own best interests at heart.

'So what's on the street, Squinty?' said Cottle, pouring a measure of whiskey from his office bottle and offering it across his desk. 'I hear we have visitors in town.'

'You bet, Mr Cottle,' grinned Squinty, accepting the measure. 'Willard Pierce you know to. Who doesn't?' He sipped the drink, closed his eyes, tilted his head to one side and murmured, 'Vintage Kentucky. I know a Kentucky when I savour it.' He sipped again. 'But it isn't Pierce who's rousing the interest. It's Jones.'

'Jones?' said Cottle cocking an interested eyebrow. 'And just who is Jones?'

'Ah,' gestured Squinty with the half-empty glass, 'who indeed?' He settled his pose, placed the glass on the desk and leaned across it. 'If I mentioned the name John Bone, perhaps more notoriously known as John Denver Bone, would I be rousing your interest, Mr Cottle?'

The sheriff eased back in his chair, steepled his fingers and grunted. 'Tell me,' he said quietly.

Squinty finished his drink, stood back, adjusted his frock coat and elaborate tie, and tapped the side of his nose. 'This might be an ongoing account, Mr Cottle. You understand?' The sheriff nodded. Squinty took a tour round the office, drew up a chair and sat down.

'Jones arrived in town looking like a dog's dinner gone bad,' he began, with a pronounced sniff. 'Worst case of desert stink I've smelled in years.' He grimaced, eased his glass delicately across the desk, refilled it, and continued: 'Made straight for the Pearl, grabbed old Soakes behind the bar and demanded — in a real nasty way, Mr Cottle — that he deliver a message to Pierce, who at that time was in a private room meeting with no less than our own Julius Catch.' Squinty looked lovingly at the empty glass, lifted his eyes and pronounced: 'And minutes later, Mr Cottle, Jones has the freedom of the town. Can take what he wants: drinks, food, clothes, boots . . . and girls I shouldn't wonder when he's had a bath, which he's doing right now. And all on the guarantee of Willard Pierce.'

Squinty sampled the replenished glass of whiskey in a single gulp and slumped in the chair. He gulped again and murmured, 'I'm telling you, Mr Cottle, we ain't never seen anything like it in Remedy before, and it does not bode well. No sir, it does not.'

Sheriff Cottle waited a moment, collapsed his steepled fingers and placed his hands flat on the desk. 'So how come in all this that Mr Jones happens, in your opinion, to be John Denver Bone?'

'Memory, Mr Cottle, pure memory,' smiled Squinty. 'Remember the time I was out Brelladose way at my Aunt Rosie's funeral — God rest her soul — well, it was there I saw this poster, clear as day on the sheriff's notice board: John Denver Bone. And he's here, with the blessing no less, of Willard Pierce. I ain't mistaken. I never am. And definitely not where killers, rapists and robbers are concerned. You can bet your last Kentucky to that!'

# 18

Remedy lapsed into a state of shadowy unease for what remained of that day until sundown. Jones and his sudden lease into free-spending on whatever and wherever he chose among the town's trades folk, was viewed at first with some mirth and curiosity. Then, as the day wore on, with an increasing sense of foreboding as the man wended his way down the main street like a drunk at a rancher's hoedown.

Pierce's sidekick, Coe, was never far behind him, noting every move, every purchase, listening to every word the man uttered. As was Squinty Poult, shifting, ducking and diving faster than an angry fly. 'Don't lose sight of the fella,' Cottle had ordered. 'But say nothin' of your suspicions about him bein' Denver Bone.'

It was not until the first lanterns had

been lit and the evening closed in that Jones finally retired to a room at the Pearl Saloon. Meantime, Willard Pierce and the town banker had ordered a lavish dinner, the best whiskey and selected themselves some suitable female company and settled themselves, it seemed, for a comfortable night. Coe took up a place in a corner of the bar. Squinty scribbled away at his endless notes in a black-backed book between visits to the street, the saloon and the sheriff's office. By nine o'clock he was resigned to a long, hot night in which, he fancied, there would be little chance of sleep.

It was ten o'clock with the street quiet, the bar in a sober mood, when Doc Parker hurried from the far end of town in search of Frank Cottle.

'Just been tendin' Mrs Kent's latest confinement,' he wheezed once on the veranda to the office. He swallowed, caught his breath, and went on. 'And guess what? You won't. We got more strangers in town. Five men, one of them gettin' on some, and one I'd

171

swear is that sonofa-mountain-bitch Reece. Holed up in them ruined barns back of the Kent spread. Arrived an hour ago. So what the hell's goin' on in this town, Frank? Why the sudden popularity of the place? Damn it, we're attractin' folk faster than flies to a bucket of dung.'

But that was the whole trouble. Cottle had no idea what was going on. No notion. Not an inkling. Right then, in the cooler air of the deep black night, he was literally in the dark.

'Job for Squinty, I reckon,' said Doc.

* * *

The Kent spread, a half-mile short of town, was a sprawl of home, paddock, corral, tumbledown shacks and barns where Lenny Kent and his wife Sue had raised their brood of six — the seventh due any day — in a clean, caring, atmosphere where all played their part in producing a living. There were no claims to fancy styles out at the Kent spread, and no secrets.

But there were hiding places. And Reece had found exactly what he had been looking for . . .

'We stay low. No swagger out there. I wanna know where Pierce is, what he plans, and if that rat Jones is anywhere around,' Reece had announced once he, his sidekicks, Charlie and Holden were settled in the dark of an old barn. 'The boys here, and you, Mr Holden will ride into town, take stock, see and hear what you can. And in case you're gettin' wild thoughts, Holden, you try anythin' or not show up, your friend Deakin here is crow meat. I do not fool.'

Twenty minutes later Charlie watched Reece's men and Holden head for town.

\* \* \*

Lemuel Buthnott had never taken to horses. He disliked their appearance, could not understand their temperament and was a totally incompetent rider. Most horses, in their turn, felt

173

much the same about the storekeeper. And so he had spent his life trying to avoid them. Not easy in a world where the horse was second only to God.

But on this day he had no choice. Sangro and his men joined now by Madelaine Pierce, were calling all the shots. And they were riding fast and hard, the dust and dirt swirling round and behind them as if caught in a whirlwind, their mounts lathered, tack jangling furiously, hard-baked leather creaking menacingly, the pound of hoofs rolling out across that scorched wilderness like the steady beat of war drums.

Sangro's plan was to come within a few miles of Remedy, rein up and select a scouting party to assess and report back on the situation in town.

'We shall be looking for specific faces and listening up for the mood of the place,' Madelaine Pierce had announced like a general on parade astride his mount. 'We are not for delaying what's to be done when the time is right. We shall ride hard as we can till the horses need water. No stopping for anything. Understood?'

No one had questioned her authority. Perhaps no one had dared to, thought Buthnott, watching her now as she rolled easily to the pace of her mount, her stare focused and steady on the distance ahead, her mind doubtless filled with only her determination to seek out revenge on her husband. And help herself to the spoils.

But where would Sangro fit in? Be a pliable, willing means to Madelaine Pierce's ultimate goal, or would he simply play her game till the spoils were in reach, then change the rules? And what of Reece? Where and when would he step back into the picture; more importantly in what sort of mood?

Buthnott winced and cursed the sheer agony of being perched in a saddle. What too of Mr Jones, and what fate had Charlie Deakin and Holden faced in Reece's hands? Where were they?

The questions raced, the images

flared and died like flames, and not for the first time since leaving Harper's Town he felt the horrible chill through his sweat of worse things to come.

He blinked the dust from his eyes and went back to watching Madelaine Pierce.

★ ★ ★

There was no more than the soft glow of the lantern light in Sheriff Cottle's office when Squinty Poult entered quietly by the back door and joined the sheriff at the window overlooking the now silent, empty main street.

'Quiet enough out there,' said Cottle, sampling the coffee from his tin mug. 'Help yourself. Coffee's fresh.'

Squinty poured his own drink and went back to the window.

'See anythin'?' asked the sheriff.

'Jones or Denver Bone is sleepin' it off. He's had one helluva night,' said Squinty.

'Alone?'

'Too bushed for company, I'd reckon. Pierce and Catch have long since retired. They ain't alone. Bar's all quiet. Town's for sleepin', I'd say. Mebbe a big day comin' up.'

The sheriff grunted and took another drink of his coffee. 'Any sign of them fellas Doc reckons are holed up at the Kent place?'

'Nothin' right here in town, but it'd be my figurin' that them critters won't be for showin' 'til sun-up, and mebbe later. Specially not if one of 'em really is that mountain man. Hell, what brings him this close to civilization? He ain't for towns, generally. Prefers them hills of his. And how come there's only five of 'em? Reece is for numbers, surroundin' himself with guns. This is breakin' his pattern.'

Cottle laid aside his empty mug and rubbed his chin. 'Exactly what I was thinkin', Squinty. Don't tally none, does it? In fact, nothin' round here figures and ain't done since Willard Pierce and his sidekick rode in. And that in itself begs a whole heap of questions more so since he got to treatin' Jones, or more probably Bone, like some aristocracy.' He sniffed. 'Whole thing smells.'

'You want we should get some boys out to the Kent spread?' said Squinty. 'Keep an eye on things.'

'No. Might go for raisin' trouble, and that ain't helpin' Mrs Kent in her condition.' The sheriff paused for a moment in thought. 'No, I reckon our next best move is to greet whoever Reece has sent or is bringin' with him at sun-up, if that's what he plans. And your job, Squinty, is to let me know the minute you catch so much as their breath.'

'You goin' to pull them in, Mr Cottle?' frowned Squinty.

'I'll think of somethin', don't you fret,' smiled the sheriff to himself. 'Somethin' 'in the public interest' wouldn't you reckon? Yeah, I figure so. Public interest and overall well-being . . . Now what would you reckon that to be at a time like this?'

# 19

'We split,' said Holden, his eyes glinting through the darkness. 'Be light in under the hour. Splittin' up will be the safest. Look a whole sight more natural than three of us ridin' in.'

The thicker-set of the two sidekicks spat and glared darkly from where he lounged in the cover with his back to the rocks. 'That ain't so smart from where I'm standin', mister,' he growled. 'Supposin' you keep ridin' straight on out of here? Nothin' to stop you.'

'There's Deakin back there with Reece,' said Holden, his stare steady. 'I ain't for desertin' him.'

The second sidekick hitched his pants. 'So what's your plan?'

'You two ride in from this end of the town. Get yourself breakfast at the saloon. Stay quiet. Listen to the talk. Watch for Jones and maybe even Pierce.

Sit real easy. Relaxed. Don't draw attention to yourselves.'

'And you?' asked the sidekick. 'What will you be doin'?'

'I'll wait a while the other side of town, then move in. But we don't meet up. Not 'til I give the word or one of you learns somethin' Reece needs to know. We don't leave town 'til we've got all we want from it.' Holden cupped a flaring match in his hands and lit a small cheroot. He let the smoke drift for a moment, then added. 'And you got my word on it I won't pull out. Just goin' to have to trust me, boys. No other choice.'

He smiled behind the curling smoke.

\* \* \*

Sheriff deputies, Mart Sykes and Will Short, were waiting in the saloon bar when the two strangers pushed open the batwings and crossed to a small table in the corner and ordered breakfasts.

'Full as they come, fella,' called the

thick-set man to the barman.

'Comin' up, boys. Ain't none fuller.'

The deputies waited until the two men had settled to their meals before crossing to their table.

'Goin' to have to relieve you of your sidearms, fellas,' said Sykes, shifting his weight to one leg. 'Sheriff's orders.'

'Since when?' scowled the leaner of the two. 'We ain't here for no trouble.'

'Law's the law,' said Will Short. 'Orders is orders.'

'Go hang your orders, mister,' grunted the thickset man, his cheeks fat with food, his jaws chewing like a longhorn. 'We ain't for givin' up our pieces to nobody, not here, not nowhere.'

The deputies exchanged quick glances. The barman polished a glass that was already sparkling. Proprietor of the Pearl, Sam Anders, closed the door to his private room without so much as a click of the catch, pulled nervously at his embroidered waistcoat and left the cigar in his fingers unlit. He swallowed and waited.

'You sure about that?' asked deputy Sykes. 'Quite sure?'

'We've said, ain't we?' said the leaner man, laying aside his fork and leaning back. 'You want it spelled out or somethin'?' he grinned.

'No need,' snapped Will Short, a Colt gleaming in his right hand. 'Just put your pieces on the table real slow, nice and easy, and get to your feet. Both of you. Now!'

The sidekicks stared, torn between drawing their guns and Reece's orders.

'Have it your way, fella,' said the thick-set man with a sigh of resignation as he released his gunbelt. 'But I warn you now, pair of you, you're goin' to regret this. And how!'

\* \* \*

'You've got two, but there's three of 'em rode in,' said Squinty Poult, dusting down his frock coat without shifting his glinting gaze from Sheriff Cottle's bottle of vintage Kentucky whiskey.

'And the third's still here,' he added with a calculated lift of his eyebrows.

'Where?' croaked Cottle, sliding an untouched mug of early morning coffee to his desk. 'You seen him? *Where* is he, Squinty?'

'Out the back,' smiled Squinty, clutching the lapels of his coat. 'Waitin' on you. Says he wants to see you.'

'*Out the back*,' gasped the sheriff. 'What the hell's he doin'?'

'Don't worry. He ain't no threat, but he figures it wouldn't be discreet right now to be seen in your office, specially not by the scum you got penned. Go see for yourself. But I warn you, you're in for a surprise.'

Cottle gulped. 'Yeah . . . yeah, I will . . . I'll go see him.' He turned, then turned again. 'Help yourself to a whiskey — just one.'

★ ★ ★

For Charlie Deakin it had been a long, taut night. And first light had brought little change. Reece still paced between brooding moodily and watching Charlie as if shooting him then and there was becoming increasingly difficult to resist. Charlie had thought once that he might have been dozing, but the merest scuff of a boot had brought the man awake and his eyes wide faster than a cat sensing a straying mouse.

Charlie had lapsed into a jumble of thoughts tracing him from leaving Harper's Town to his present dilemma like free-falling from a mountainside. He had been glad to see the first wink of dawn. 'Holden's takin' his time,' he said, watching from the side of an open window as the light stained the eastern skies. 'Mebbe he ain't got so lucky. Mebbe — '

'He knows the stakes,' grunted Reece, stretching his arms and flexing his legs. 'Leastways, he'd better for your sake.'

Charlie swallowed quietly and turned his attention back to the gathering light. 'Them homesteaders out there'll be stirring about now,' he murmured, peering closer at the darker spread of the ranch house, where a light glowed fitfully at a front window. 'There's stock to feed. Horses. Brood of young 'uns too. I heard 'em in the night. Lively bunch by the sound of 'em.'

Reece stretched again. 'They ain't no trouble to us, mister. They come this way and . . . well, I ain't for reckonin' on that. You just keep your eyes peeled for Holden or one of my boys. Your future depends on it.'

Charlie had ignored Reece's sardonic grin and kept his gaze fixed on what was happening beyond their cover of the tumbledown barn. There was no visible movement yet among the homesteaders, but there was movement. Somebody out there. Somebody keeping awful quiet and staying very low. And he was not, by Charlie's reckoning, interested in the ranch house, the stock or the corral. No, if anything he was heading towards the barn.

Now who on earth might that be at

this godforsaken hour of a fresh-cut morning when the lure of a blanket pulled close up to the chin would have been a whole sight more appealing.

Charlie relaxed. Maybe he would not have to wait long to find out.

★ ★ ★

Sheriff Cottle sank his second large whiskey of the morning and sat back in his chair with a decidedly bewildered look glazing his tired eyes.

'I ain't heard nothin' like it in a lifetime of law-keepin',' he said slowly, deeply as if counting out the words. 'In fact, I ain't never heard anythin' like it no time, no place and, sonofa-goddam-bitch, I doubt if I ever will.'

'Me neither,' murmured Doc Parker.

'Same here,' added Squinty to the nodding of Cottle's deputies.

'Talk about takin' the biscuit,' Cottle continued. 'This needs the whole darned tin! And it's all gatherin' right here, in my town; here in the streets of

Remedy.' He thought about another whiskey, thought better of it and lit a cheroot instead. 'Just reckon it . . . '

'I am,' said Doc, 'and I'll tell you what we've got.' Doc raised a hand and began to tick off his list one by one. 'We've got Willard Pierce, and how! From what the sheriff here has been told by Holden perhaps the all-time fraudster and con man, not to mention out-and-out robber and scum this territory — any *other* territory come to that — has ever witnessed.'

Sheriff Cottle sighed. The deputies simply stared at Doc. Squinty adjusted his frock coat and, on the nod from Cottle, helped himself to another Kentucky whiskey.

Doc stiffened his shoulders and continued, 'Then we have Mr Jones — in reality the notorious gunslingin' outlaw, murderer and rapist, Denver Bone.' Doc grunted officiously. 'But we ain't done yet — oh, no, not by a long shot. Next on our list is Reece, the lowest of the lowest, robbin', kidnappin' and God alone knows what else, mountain gang leader, complete, I should add, with his whole stinkin' crowd of gunslingers waitin' on his word to hit Remedy like a tornado.'

Doc paused to catch his breath and without hesitation or approval from the sheriff, pour himself a large drink.

'But I ain't done yet. You bet,' he grinned. 'No sir. We then have Mr Holden, source of all this information. He's here no less than to kill Denver Bone. How don't matter. Shootin', stabbin', hangin' . . . any one'll do. Holden is, in fact, Marshal Holden, retired now, but Bone has been the burr in his boot for more years than he cares to remember. And he ain't settlin' to no rocker 'til Denver Bone is brought to law.'

Doc paused again to finish his whiskey and add quietly. 'And all this, gentlemen, the result of Willard Pierce and one of the most outrageous stage hold-ups it's been my misfortune to hear. Don't bear thinkin' to, none of it.'

He finished, laid aside his empty glass, and stared at Sheriff Cottle who drew deeply on his cheroot, came to his feet and crossed to the office window. 'Holden's headed back to the Kent spread right now,' he said coldly. 'Pierce is sleepin' at the Pearl. Bone doin' likewise. We move in a half-hour, first to — '

'Ain't you forgettin' somethin' here?' asked Squinty, reckoning that the whiskey bottle offered one more measure.

'And what's that?' asked Doc.

'Mrs Pierce. I hear she's still out there some place captive of Reece's men. There's some fella along of her. But how long are them mountain scum goin' to wait before movin'? More to the point, how long's Mrs Pierce goin' to wait?'

# 20

Denver Bone twitched the drapes aside carefully, stared into the street, left to right, back again, and smiled softly to himself. It had all worked like cracking cackle-berries to a plains' trail pan. Darn near perfect. And now there was hardly a soul about, the street was empty save for the dawn risers and hungover drunks. And the day was his to do with as he wished.

He stepped back from the window and viewed himself in the room's full-length mirror. Smart, he thought, adjusting the set of his shirt collar. In keeping with the man he was. His new clothes — courtesy of Willard Pierce — had an edge, a style, same as the fellow wearing them. No more Mr Jones! No more ten days' stubble and dirt; no more shabby pants, worn boots; no more looking like a two-bit drifter. And he had a pair of brand new, tool-handled Colts to grace his sides, a blade in his boot, and a hat, dark, broad brimmed, set low, to give him the shade from which to stare without necessarily being seen.

Denver Bone was back, alive and straining at the leash to get his hands on the fortune just waiting to be lifted. If he was quick enough.

He turned to the window again, twitched the drapes and scanned the still sleeping street. He grunted softly. His ruse the night before to feign that he was boozed fit to sleep a week had been another success. There would be no one bothering to even try to wake the guest in Room Eight. Mr Jones was not to be disturbed as he had so explicitly ordered.

Two minutes later, Denver Bone, alias Mr Jones, had slipped quietly from his room to the balcony overlooking the saloon bar, checked that all was quiet and slid away through the back door to the stairway that led to a side alley.

Once there, he paused, took stock again and moved away in the direction of the town's rooming-house where its only resident should be stirring to begin his day.

His last.

★ ★ ★

Squinty Poult, on the other hand, had different ideas about Denver Bone's behaviour the previous night, though he had said nothing to those who had witnessed the man's bar room shenanigans and generosity. Squinty had long since come to realize that sealed lips in his profession were sometimes worth a whole sight more than a loose mouth. And so he had kept to himself his opinion that Mr Jones was no more drunk than a Bible-punching cleric preaching abstinence when the man had finally staggered to his room.

And now, here in the early morning light at the rear of the Pearl Saloon he was waiting his chance to prove it.

He watched Bone hesitate, look round, listen, then begin to work his way through the clutter of crates, barrels, timbers, broken shacks and sheds. Squinty followed. When it came to shadowing a fellow, Squinty was one of the best. He went uncannily lightly and silently on his feet for a man of his age; he could judge distance and staying close to a hair's-breadth. He was, in effect, a shadow of the man he was following.

Bone halted, peered from the cover of a leaning shed door. Squinty waited, watched, narrowed his eyes. No hint of a hangover with this fellow, he thought, behind a soft grin. And he seemed to know exactly where he was heading.

Bone moved on again, this time at a slightly brisker pace. Feeling confident, reckoned Squinty, increasing his own pace; the man was anxious now to be through with whatever it was he had in mind.

It was another three minutes, however, before Squinty finally realized just where they were heading: Ma Crew's rooming-house, back of the bank. And she had only one guest right now: Willard Pierce's side-kick, Coe. Hell, thought Squinty, Bone was for meeting up with him. To what end, he wondered; joining up with Pierce, bringing some sort of message; maybe he had been a part of the conspiracy from the start? After all, he had shown up in town from nowhere, seemingly alone and Pierce had seen him and lavished money on him without question.

Bone came to the last of the shacks and clutter before the open space to the rooming-house's neat picket fence enclosing a tended garden. He waited, watching the house, scanning the windows in his view. Could be he was looking for a sign, a presence, thought Squinty. Seconds later, Bone was gone again, moving fast over the open ground, no hesitation, direct to the front porch, the few steps to the smoked-glass fronted doors, through them and into the sprawling hall, with its leather armchairs and mahogany side table where Ma Crew would be with her ready smile all set to welcome her early visitor.

Squinty swallowed, mopped his sticky brow. What to do? Should he follow Bone or go summon the sheriff? Did he have the time? No time, he decided. The only thing he could safely do was give it a few minutes and follow into the house, then find whatever he might find or have to face.

★   ★   ★

He found what he had half-expected.

Ma Crew had been tied to her kitchen chair, bound and gagged by her own kitchen towels.

'Cheek of the devil!' she glowered, adjusting her dress over her ample bosom. 'Lord above knows what he was after. Just wanted to know Mr Coe's room, then disappeared. Tied me here and went.'

'You were lucky,' said Squinty.

'Bah!' fumed Ma, with a slap of the air. '*He* got lucky more like! Twenty years ago I'd have had him trussed faster than he could spit, and a good hidin' to follow!'

'Well, mebbe you would, Ma, but right now you stay right here, you understand? Right here, while I go see what's been happenin'. Pour yourself a glass of that whiskey I know you got stashed back there.'

'You know a heap more than is healthy for you, Squinty Poult. And I hope you've wiped your feet before you go trampin' all over my freshly cleaned carpets. If I find — '

What Squinty found in the guest's room was enough to turn his stomach at any time of day, but at this time in the morning on an empty stomach . . .

Coe had been stabbed and his throat cut exactly where he lay doubtless in a half-awake state on his bed. The man's eyes were open, fixed in a moon-like stare on the ceiling. Blood was flowing freely, dripping now at a steady pace from the bed to the carpet. Ma Crew was going to have a heap to say about this.

Squinty turned and headed back down the stairs. Hell, he thought, the day was not yet fully fledged. What in God's name was to come?

★  ★  ★

'Willard Pierce and Julius Catch are behind bars, and that's where they're stayin', damnit. Leastways 'til I've got this whole stinkin' mess cleared up and my town back to somethin' like civilized.'

Sheriff Cottle took a hold of the lapels on his waistcoat and filled his lungs with the fresher morning air, at the same time turning a defiant glare over the assembled men in the street fronting his office. He grunted, paced to the railing and stared into the still hazy morning.

'Now all you've got to do is go find

that rat who's just knifed the fella at Ma Crew's place,' said an old-timer, puffing a cloud of smoke from his corn cob pipe. 'T'ain't goin' to be easy,' he added with a noisy suck.

'I know that well enough,' said Cottle, turning back to the men. 'But the man we first knew as Mr Jones, who now turns out to be the notorious Denver Bone, will be brought to book. You can bet on it.'

'Sure he will,' piped a lanky man sporting frayed braces supporting baggy pants, 'but what about them two mountain types you're holdin', and what about the Kents — who's holed-up there; is it Reece — and who's this fella Holden, Marshal Holden no less, you been tellin' us about? Where's it all headin', Sheriff?'

The gathering murmured its agreement.

'We in real danger here, Mr Cottle?' called a man.

'What about the women and kids?' said another.

'Town's fast fillin' with gunslingers and scum,' added a third.

'This is a territorial matter,' a fourth man called. 'Mebbe the army.'

'Now hold it right there,' shouted Cottle above the suddenly clamouring voices. 'You're lettin' this situation get out of proportion.'

'Not from where I'm standin' we ain't,' chipped a shirt-sleeved man with a cheroot wedged in the corner of his mouth.

'S'right, Sheriff,' said the fellow with braces. 'Situation seems clear enough to me; town's gettin' to heave with no-gooders, and it ain't none of our makin'. We didn't start all this, f'Chris'sake. We just happen to be right in the path of a hurricane, and there don't look to be no easy escape.'

Doc Parker stepped to the sheriff's side, raised his arms and called for quiet. 'That's far enough,' he ordered, waiting for the voices to fall silent. 'We ain't goin' nowhere with this sort of talk. I'm sure Sheriff Cottle here knows what he's doin' and how its got to be done for the benefit and safety of all of us. So now here's what I propose.' The men gave him their full attention. 'I propose we offer to help the sheriff and his deputies in the best way we can. The only way we're goin' to come through this anythin' like unscathed is by stickin' t'gether. Workin' t'gether. So, who's for volunteerin'? Step forward those ready to stand to Sheriff Cottle's side . . . '

* * *

Charlie shifted his right boot deliberately through the dry straw of the barn floor. It was a noise fit to stir a spider — and it did — or even a mouse. He smiled as he watched the little varmint scurry away towards the dozing bulk of Reece. 'But f'Chris'sake don't wake him,' hissed Charlie to himself. 'Not now . . . '

He glanced across the empty ground to where he had last seen the shadow closing, then again at Reece. God willing the rat would stay sleeping for at least another couple of minutes, maybe three, five at the outside, just long enough for whoever was out there to make it across the last twenty yards.

He wiped a trickle of sweat from his cheek, ran a hand round his damp, sticky neck, adjusted his hat and narrowed his eyes. Could be, of course, that the shadow was one of Reece's sidekicks; could be he was a town man. Could be he was the sheriff . . .

He swallowed, sweated, saw a face.

'What kept you?' he croaked on a hiss of breath as Holden moved towards him, a Colt already fixed in his grip. 'Lookin' for Reece? He's right here. Sleepin'.' Charlie turned to see a space where only seconds before Reece had been sleeping. 'Leastways, he was . . . '

# 21

The first shot spat like sudden flame, missing Charlie's shoulder by a hair's-breadth. He flung himself to his left, crashing into a pile of feed sacks, two crates and loose timbers. It was the cover of this mayhem that saved him as Reece's second shot blazed uselessly into a chunk of wood.

'What the hell!' gasped Charlie, floundering among the sacks and crates, feeling the crush of the timbers and then realizing that they were, in fact, his life-saving cover. He lay perfectly still, not daring to so much as swallow.

Silence. Then a movement. Back of the barn.

Another movement, this time from the far side. Reece at the back, wondered Charlie, Holden circling him, watching, waiting?

Suddenly a voice. 'Seems like you're on your own, Holden,' growled Reece. 'You dump my boys or did you shoot 'em? One or the other, I'll bet.' He tittered. 'Well, I guess I ain't surprised. Should've known you'd try somethin'. My big mistake. Figure I'll just have to put matters right, eh? Redeem the situation.'

Reece fired blindly, hoping to flush his prey from the shadows. No such luck. Holden was having none of it. Charlie smiled to himself. Set a tiger to kill a tiger . . .

Reece's voice growled again: 'Them boys of mine were no big deal, anyhow,' he sneered cynically. 'Got a whole sight better ridin' alongside Sangro. And when he gets here, mister, you can bet we'll take this town apart plank by plank if we have to. We sure as hell won't be leavin' without that bankin' fortune stashed right where we want it. And a whole heap of dead bodies behind us. Just like we love it! Beginnin' with you, mister! How about that, eh?'

He blazed a shot wildly, his aim loose into the shadowy space, his hope once again to flush Holden into moving. One small sound, one step would be enough for the eagle-eyed Reece.

Silence! Nothing moved.

Charlie swallowed, licked at cold sweat. Winced at the growing weight of the timbers covering him. Goddamn it, he thought, he had forgotten entirely about the oncoming threat of Sangro. When would he hit town? How far from Remedy was he now? Were Madelaine Pierce and Buthnott still with him? How many were riding out there? The whole miserable, trail-stinking bunch, you could bet. He cursed quietly under his breath and went back to listening.

Still all quiet, as if the morning here in Remedy had come to a halt, suspended in its own time, waiting for a sky-rolling storm to finally break. A sharp, impatient intake of breath.

Reece was beginning to fidget; maybe feeling the creeping tingle of uncertainty. He had no notion of Holden's abilities, his techniques, if any. But he could sense he already had the edge.

'That's enough, Holden,' snapped Reece. 'I ain't got the time or inclination to be messin' further with you. I'm comin' out.'

He threw a length of broken timber to his left and stepped quickly from the shadow to the softer light to his right, his Colt already steady at waist level and blazing a single shot directly ahead of him.

And that is where he was duped.

'This side, Reece,' said Holden as his form took shape only inches from where Reece had tossed the broken timber.

Reece swung round, a snarl on his suddenly sweat-soaked face, his eyes wide and wet and staring. 'Rat!' he cursed, but had no time to fire again as Holden's Colt blazed three times in quick succession, crumpling Reece's body to the dusty floor where blood soaked instantly into the dry straw and three flies swooped from nowhere.

'You can come out now, Charlie,' called Holden, arming his Colt again from his gunbelt.

★ ★ ★

Alvin Rook had been Remedy's storekeeper for more than twenty years. Of late, along with Sheriff Cottle, Doc Parker and the Pearl Saloon's proprietor, Sam Anders, he had also come to be regarded as a town elder and unofficial and unelected mayor.

It was in his civic capacity that he had spent the early part of that morning discussing the events at Ma Crew's rooming-house with the sheriff, Squinty and Doc, and that, in turn, had led to the late opening of the store. Something he did not condone, not even to himself in spite of pressing circumstances.

Fact was, Denver Bone was a danger, a killer, a notorious gunman at large in Remedy and had to be penned as soon as possible. That Willard Pierce had been about to use the town as his final escape route after pillaging the funds of his own bank, was headache enough. But now Sheriff Cottle was speaking of other 'difficulties' looming. The morning, he had decided, was already a nightmare.

And now here he was late opening by close on forty minutes.

He checked his timepiece again, grunted, pocketed it and unlocked the store with a flourish. Order of priorities were: shutters up, dusting all through in twenty minutes, stocks replenished where necessary, candy jar refilled, coffee all set to brew, and then, and only then . . .

He saw no one, heard nothing, not a footfall, the squeak of a floor board, until the voice spoke behind the ominous click of a gun hammer and the closing of the door.

'Not a sound, mister,' hissed Denver Bone, stepping to the storekeeper's back. He prodded the gun barrel into Rook's ribs. 'Just step quietly to that counter there and listen real close to what I've got to say. You don't miss a word. Understood? One mistake and you're crow meat. And I do not mess.'

'You won't get away with this. I'll see you — ' spluttered Rook.

'I said not a word, didn't I?' hissed Bone again. 'So that's your first mistake. Don't make another. Just listen.'

* * *

'Now what?' said Squinty Poult, pressing closer to the window in Sheriff Cottle's office. He rubbed a pane clear of dust and haze and squinted. 'Alvin Rook, hurryin' this way lookin' like he's just seen a ghost ... And in his shirt sleeves at that. Alvin never crosses the street without his jacket. So what's eatin' him?'

Sheriff Cottle crossed to the door, opened it and moved to the boardwalk just as Alvin reached the steps, his face gleaming with sweat, his eyes as round as new moons.

'What's got to you, Alvin?' frowned the sheriff. 'You look — '

'Inside. Inside,' urged the store-keeper, shooing Cottle back to his office.

Squinty and the sheriff waited the few minutes it took for Rook to sink a measure of whiskey, catch his breath, mop his face and sink exhausted into a chair.

'Denver Bone . . . He's back there, in the store. Was waitin' on me. Says he'll torch the place and half the town with it if you don't do exactly as he says.'

The sheriff waited again while Rook sank his second whiskey, then asked, 'So what's he demandin'?'

The storekeeper mopped his brow. 'The release no less of Willard Pierce and Julius Catch and a guaranteed safe passage out of town when the three of them are good and ready.' Rook gulped. 'Got his eyes on the main chance, ain't he? He wants a share of that bank heist. He figures on freein' Pierce as the way to a personal fortune. That's why he killed Coe at the roomin'-house, and that's sure as snow in winter why he'll do what he says if we don't shift. And fast!'

Rook came to his feet. 'I've got to get back, otherwise he'll start . . . Hell, it don't bear thinkin' to. So what's your answer, Sheriff? What do I tell the rat?'

★   ★   ★

'You had no choice, none at all,' said Doc Parker quietly, laying a hand on Sheriff Cottle's arm. 'We'd all have done the same thing. There's too much at stake. Too many lives that might be lost. So uselessly.'

'But you've stalled things some,' added Squinty, scanning the street from the office window. 'You don't have to be in a mad dog hurry to set them scum free. Make Bone wait twenty minutes, anyhow. Give us time to think things through.'

The sheriff lit a fresh cheroot and blew an anxious stream of smoke. 'Ain't a lot of thinkin' to be done now, is there? Pierce is goin' to ride free, Bone and just about anybody else of his choosin' along of him and that'll be that. We'll be left — '

'No more talk like that,' snapped Doc, pouring a measure of whiskey for Cottle. 'Let me prescribe this on medical grounds right here and now! Drink it.' He watched as the sheriff gulped the drink in one, closed his eyes, smacked his lips and smiled. 'That's better,' Doc went on. 'Now forget Pierce and anythin' else that might or might not be about to descend on this town like a clap of thunder, and figure this fella Holden, the so-called marshal. When do you reckon for him showin' his face again?'

'In about five minutes flat,' murmured Squinty from the window. 'Here he comes right now. Top of the street there. Him, an old-timer, and — Guess what, gentlemen. He's trailin' a horse back of him with a body slumped across it lookin' very dead. Yeah, I'd say so. Very dead indeed . . . '

# 22

The street was beginning to fill with groups and gatherings of townfolk by the time Holden, Charlie and the trailed mount, bearing the body of Reece, had passed the livery corral and the freshly fuelled blacksmith's forge. For an eerie moment the trio passed into a haze of smoke and were lost from sight, with only the scuff of hoofs through sand announcing their approach. Then, like ghosts, they were there again and taking on shapes. The folk watched in silence, some open-mouthed, some simply staring, others chewing slowly on baccy cud, the women staying watchful and wary.

'Ain't that the mountain rat we been tryin' to nail all these years?' asked a man in a moth-eaten straw hat.

'That's him,' answered an old-timer with a corncob pipe smouldering sweetly between his broken teeth. 'That's the scumbag who did for my best neighbour Jed Pye when him and me were out pannin' along the Chesney river beds. Sonofabitch.' The old man removed the pipe and spat fiercely. 'Good riddance to scum!'

Charlie Deakin took his eyes away from the street, the staring faces, the deep shadows, to glance anxiously at Holden. The man appeared indifferent to the street, the townfolk, even the body being trailed; it might have been a sack of beans for all he cared. That, of course, as Charlie well knew by now, was not the case. You could bet your last cent, he thought, that Holden's seemingly indifferent gaze had not missed so much as the shift of a boot, the lift of a finger.

'Keep movin', Mr Deakin,' said the man quietly. 'Dead ahead to the sheriff's office. We ain't concerned — '

It was the crashing open of the double doors to Alvin Rook's store that spooked Holden's mount into a sudden snort and lurch as Denver Bone strode to the boardwalk, a levelled Colt in each hand, and sneered at the approaching riders.

'That's far enough, Mr Holden,' he called. 'You can ease up right there, and don't move a muscle.'

Holden and Charlie did as ordered, reining their frisky mounts to a halt in a swirl of dust.

'And you folk off the street if you want to stay breathin',' snapped Denver Bone. 'I'll shoot the first dumb-head who so much as thinks of goin' for a gun. So shift. Now!' He gestured menacingly with the Colts, then turned his glare back on Holden and Charlie.

'You've been real busy there, Mr Holden,' he sneered. 'Takin' charge, eh? Assumed your rightful role — Marshal Holden!' He twirled a Colt flamboyantly. 'Think I didn't figure for who you were? Got you soon out of Harper's Town. But I didn't reckon you for bein' no threat — leastways not one I couldn't handle. And that still applies,

Marshal, so from here on you do as I say.' His glare darkened. 'Don't doubt it, the pair of you.' He relaxed. 'Storekeeper,' he called over his shoulder. 'You get out here right now. No messin'.'

Rook staggered from the depths of the store, his arms, bound at the wrists, waving uselessly in front of him, a trickle of blood sliding into a gathering stain on his collar. His face had turned grey, his eyes sunk, his flesh hanging looser as if suddenly deprived of its blood flow. He shuddered as he gazed over the emptying street where men and the scatterings of women were shuffling away from sight, not one of them daring to raise a word, let alone an arm, of resistance.

'Right,' said Bone. 'Now you, Holden, and you, Deakin, drop your weapons to the dirt, go hitch that scum body you're cartin' and you walk in a straight line to where that sheriff's waitin' on you and you tell him I want Pierce released right now. And you, Holden, bring him to me.'

\* \* \*

Holden and Charlie made a slow, scuffing way towards the sheriff's office where already Pierce was being held between two burly deputies, while Cottle himself, Squinty Poult and Doc Parker looked on in silence.

'And let me just remind you, Marshal Holden,' called Bone from the boardwalk, 'you put one foot wrong and the storekeeper here dies and this mercantile goes up in flames. You hearin' me there?'

'I'm hearin' you,' answered Holden without looking back.

They reached the office; Charlie hitched the trailed mount carrying the body of Reece, then spat fiercely into the dirt. 'Of all the low-down scumbags I ever had the misfortune to carry aboard one of my stage runs, darned if Denver-sonofabitch-Bone don't take the neck off a bottle of tonsil-grind! I'm tellin' you, Sheriff — '

'I'm agreein' with you, Mr Deakin,'

216

said Cottle, 'but right now we've got one helluva tricky situation on our hands. I can't afford to see the townfolk suffer — nor will I — and I risk Rook's life and his store if we don't do exactly as Bone wants. A blaze is all we need! So what's your thinkin', Marshal.'

'You and your men stay right where you are,' said Holden, his expression taut, his stare dark, 'and let me handle this my way. Charlie, you stay put. Sheriff, you cover me every inch of the way 'til I hand over Pierce. Then wait. You'll know what to do when the time comes.'

'But you can't — ' began Charlie, only to be silenced by a flash of Holden's gaze.

'Step forward Pierce,' ordered Holden. 'And remember — '

'I don't need lecturin' from you, mister,' sneered Pierce. 'Just get goin', will you.' He shook himself free of the deputies and faced Sheriff Cottle. 'My thanks for your hospitality, sir,' he grinned cynically. 'But now, I fear, I must take my leave of you. Complete my business in this hole of a town and be gone. I bid you good day.'

Groups of townfolk had gathered again in the boardwalk shadows and corners of alleyways between buildings as they watched the street drama played out: Holden and Pierce making a measured way back down the street to where Bone waited with Rook slumped in misery and fear at his side.

No one dared to move as they counted out the marshal's slow, careful tread; as they saw Willard Pierce swagger arrogantly to his pace; and as Bone simply stood, the twin Colts levelled and steady, a deep smirk of satisfaction creasing his sweat lined face.

'Two stays to a tart's bustle Bone'll shoot the Marshal soon as Pierce is free,' muttered the old-timer through the gurgling spittle in his pipe bowl. 'I seen it comin', sure I did.'

Someone shushed the old man to be

quiet. 'You didn't see no such thing,' he hissed.

A clutch of bar girls had gathered at the batwings and windows of the Pearl Saloon; a horse at the livery snorted; smoke curled lazily from the forge; a handful of flies savaged newly dropped dung; a door creaked.

Squinty Poult sweated and gulped. 'I ain't takin' odds on the outcome of this,' he murmured, mopping his cheeks.

'Nobody's bettin',' said Doc Parker grimly.

Holden had come within a few yards of the store when he halted and pushed Pierce towards the boardwalk. 'He'll kill you soon as he's got what he wants,' he warned.

'No mouthin', Holden,' grinned Bone, pulling Pierce into the shadows. 'Now comes the question, Marshal, of what to do with you after all this long time of you scratchin' like a burr in my pants. Been some journey for you, ain't it? And to think it's all goin' to end right here in Remedy. And I, Mr Holden, am goin' to end it . . . '

★   ★   ★

It only needed one man to shift his weight for a board to creak; one person to clear his throat, a hitched mount to stamp a hoof to dirt, or a fly to buzz, thought Charlie, to spark Bone into pulling the trigger and shooting Marshal Holden clean between the eyes or any other part of his anatomy. And when that killing was done, Charlie would be next. He would never live to see the subsequent carnage.

Charlie took in the street scene left to right from the corner of his eyes. Still the lazy curl of smoke from the forge; still the faces in the shadows, rows of staring eyes: the bar girls framed like something exotic in a window display where they stood framed in the batwings; the sheriff and his deputies stood watching, mute and immobile, too tensed, too aware of the knife-edge on which Holden's life was balanced for just a few more perilous seconds.

'Put the gun down, mister, before I blast you to a thousand pieces.'

It was a long half-minute before anyone seemed aware that a voice had cracked across the thick morning heat-haze.

Then slowly, deliberately, faces turned to the drift of smoke at the forge, to where a handful of roughneck, gunslinging riders fixed their gazes on the street, their sidearms drawn and levelled, rifles at the ready. At the head of them, Sangro a little to her left, sat Madeline Pierce, her broad-brimmed hat pulled low over tied-back hair, her body smooth and shapely in tight pants and shirt, a Winchester steady in her grip.

'Don't nobody move,' said the woman, menacing the rifle, her gaze moving over the townfolk, narrowing on the shadows. She paused a second longer at the sight of the marshal then quickly shifted to where Bone was lounging with his weight on one hip, his weapons at his feet.

'Well, now,' he grinned, eyes sparkling, 'look what we got — the once pampered wife of the all-time bank robber.' Pierce shot him an angry glance. 'And lookin' real good too, backed there by them scumlickin' rats you got for company.' Bone folded his arms. 'Mornin', ma'am,' he smiled. 'And what can we be doin' for you, or are you just joinin' the party?'

Sangro spat. His sidekicks sat their mounts without moving. The townfolk swallowed. Squinty Poult leaned closer to whisper in Sheriff Cottle's ear: 'What you goin' to do?' The sheriff remained silent, his stare unblinking.

'Nothin',' said Doc Parker to Squinty's surprise at being overheard.

'Willard,' called the woman, 'you just get here. Now.' She levelled the rifle at the banker. 'Start walkin'.'

Pierce stepped from the boardwalk and began the hot, dusty walk to face his wife at the livery forge. A smile had broken across his face where the stubble was darkening and the blemishes of age beginning to show.

'My dear Madelaine,' he began with excessive hand gestures, 'I'd thought . . . dreaded never seeing you again. I mean I know it looked pretty bad back there at the stage, and you must have been shocked . . . understandably so . . . at what you saw and heard. But you see, my dear, there'd been no time to prepare you, for us to plan together, though I knew . . . oh, yes, I knew . . . you'd see everything for what it was. You always did. You're smart, Madelaine, and I respect you for that. No, I love you for it. And all that I've done for you . . . for us to be together. There's money here, sure enough, at the bank. But the real wealth . . . *gold* . . . worth a fortune, is out there in the desert. And only I know where, Madelaine. So why don't you come with me now, grab ourselves some fresh horses and ride? Any place you say. Just name it. And we can begin right now. It's only a matter of — '

Madelaine Pierce began emptying the

rifle into her husband when he was just five yards away. Her first shots threw him, swirled and twirled him until it seemed he was performing some sort of ritual war dance. Then he staggered; to the left, the right, each stagger propelled through its motion by a hail of bullets blazing deliberately, unstoppably from the levelled rifle in the woman's firm grip. His face registered every known emotion of surprise, astonishment, pain, until it was no more than a twisted ball of skin and bone in which two eyes stared hopelessly at everything and nothing.

When he finally fell, spreadeagled on his back in the gritty dirt, his wife reined her mount to his side and emptied the last of the bullets into his already lifeless blood-soaked body. Then she threw the weapon across him, hailed to Sangro and the side-kicks and rode hell-for-leather clear of the town down the trail that had brought her.

Willard Pierce was no more and neither, it seemed, was his widow.

# 23

Charlie Deakin turned from the open double doors of the stage office at Harper's Town, glanced at the clock on the wall and crossed to the empty bench at the far end of the room.

'Then what?' said the young man seated on the bench opposite him. 'I mean, then what happened?'

Charlie smiled at the fellow, took a cheroot from his pocket and slowly lit it. He watched the other passengers from behind the curling cloud of smoke. To the young man's left sat a prim, neatly dressed lady who, though not yet elderly, had seen the best of more youthful years. She wore an elaborately decorated fruit and flower hat that adorned her head like a circular garden. Her eyes were blue and keen and interested. She had seen life, decided Charlie.

To the right of the young man sat a thick-set, paunchy fellow sporting a broad-brimmed cattleman's hat, an elaborate timepiece on a heavy chain strung across his stomach as if to fence off the big country, and highly polished, tooled leather boots.

'Sure,' said the cattleman, mopping his sweating face with a spotted bandanna, 'you can't just leave the story there, Mr Deakin. Damnit, fella, you were there. You saw it all.'

Charlie turned his gaze to where Merv Hinks appeared buried in a mound of ledgers, timetables and forms. 'How long we got, Mr Hinks?' he asked. 'Time to finish my story?'

Merv consulted the clock on the wall then his own timepiece. 'Last passenger will be here in ten minutes. We pull out sharp five past the hour.'

Charlie grunted, examined the glowing end of the cheroot, then turned his attention back to his waiting audience.

'So,' he began, 'what did happen? Well, like you say, mister, I was there, large as life as I am today, and saw it all. And, hell — beggin' your pardon, ma'am — was that some sight to behold . . .

'I reckon there wasn't a soul standin' in that street who wasn't fixed in the head by what he'd just witnessed. Why, you could almost smell the tension on them sweaty faces . . . just, folks, like I could smell my own right then.'

Charlie paused, drew on his cheroot, glanced at the clock and went on: 'Anyhow, long and the short of it was that Mrs Pierce and them scumbag mountain men rode out, and for what seemed a long, awful silence everybody just stood there, not movin', not speakin', not so much as breathin', I'd guess, if you'd happened to be close enough. It was one of them flouncy bar-girls who finally broke it. And how . . .'

Charlie examined his cheroot again, blew gently on the glowing tip and lifted his eyes beneath raised brows. 'She screamed. Goddamnit, of all things, she screamed! And from there on everythin' happened at once.'

Charlie paused to study the faces watching him. Merv dipped his pen in a bottle of ink, scratched a few lines across a page, dipped again and consulted the clock. Charlie took the hint and continued his story:

'Suddenly the boardwalks were alive with town folk; seemed like they came out of the woodwork. And the noise — hell, you couldn't hear yourself think! Sheriff Cottle, Squinty Poult, Doc Parker and the deputies were into the full glare of the street in seconds, their target only one man: Denver Bone. But he, not surprisingly, was already a step ahead of them. Bone had grabbed a Colt and fired in the direction of Holden and myself. Needless to say the shot was high and wild in all the mayhem. Meantime, Holden had tossed a Colt to me and collected his rifle from the dirt. 'Get into cover!' he shouted, and plunged into the store after Bone.

'Sheriff Cottle posted himself at the store and barred the way to the pressin' townfolk. 'Store's off limits', he announced. 'There's a murderin' gunslinger in there bein' pursued by a marshal. Nobody enters 'til Holden calls for assistance'. 'Or don't call at all!' snorted a wag in the crowd. Doc Parker tended Alvin Rook and despatched the deputies to seal off the saloon. 'Get them girls off the street', he said. 'And don't let the liquor start flowin' not yet awhile, anyhow. Don't want hotheads gettin' gun-happy'.

'It was then that a new kind of quiet hit the street. The folk fell silent and began to stand about again in groups. Everybody listened for the shout, the shot that must come sooner or later from inside the store. Men were shushed and told to hold their tongues; some tried to get closer; some whispered anxiously to Rook who was by now seated in the shade. Doc meanwhile had moved off to examine the body of Pierce and pronounce him dead in a tone of voice as dismissive as he could make it.'

Charlie glanced at the clock, blew a cloud of smoke and resumed his story: 'Time ticked on. The sun beat down. The heat thickened. But nobody seemed to bother. All eyes in Remedy that mornin' were concentrated on the store. And I'd wager there wasn't an ear not primed for the slightest sound.

'Then, like somethin' out of Hell itself, it came . . .

'And how! Two shots, fast, from the room above the store. I figured them from Bone's Colt. Another shot. 'That's three', quipped a fella. We waited. Sheriff Cottle's face erupted in a lathering of sweat. Doc Parker placed his bag at his feet. A woman shepherded her two children into shade. The deputies waited on the boardwalk frontin' the saloon. An old-timer lit his pipe from a slow burnin' flame. The forge smoke still curled as if it didn't give a damn.

'Holden's first blaze from the rifle

threw the dark shape of Bone back against the storeroom window over-lookin' the street. The second ripped into the body like a tornado, tossing it through the window. Glass and timber filled the air like rain, and Bone seemed to fly and stay suspended, 'til finally it fell, slowly, deliberately, like somethin' cloaked. It hit the street with a sickenin' thud and just lay there, bleedin', useless, lifeless, the eyes starin' into a cloudless blue sky. And that, folks, was the end of Denver Bone.'

'What happened to Holden?' asked the cattleman.

Charlie finished his cheroot, ground it out and eased back on the bench. 'He'd got his man after all that time and that was enough. He witnessed the burial on Remedy's Boot Hill, took on supplies and headed due West. Said he'd mebbe look in on Harper's Town someday, but not so far. The men Sheriff Cottle had jailed were duly dealt with, includin' the collaboratin' bank manager. And Remedy, I guess, settled back to its peaceful self. They'd had excitement enough!'

'But what about all that gold Pierce said he had buried in the desert?' said the young man. 'And what about Buthnott, what became of him? Did he stay with Mrs Pierce, or did she — ?'

'Easy, easy,' urged Charlie. 'One thing at a time, please.' He paused a moment. 'Madeleine Pierce and Sangro left the storekeeper right there in Remedy. Left him sweat-soaked and scared clean out of his skin. You bet! But he survived, sure he did, and he's back here in Harper's Town still building his mercantile empire, still makin' his annual trip to Rainwater, though his travellin' these days ain't nothin' like so lively! And I'll tell you what, folks, he ain't for bein' henpecked by that wife of his. Not no how he ain't. He's one helluva sight more for puttin' her right back in her place minute she gets one bit lippy. You should hear him!'

Charlie smiled. 'As for the rest, well nobody to my knowledge ever found the gold, though plenty have searched. Some do say as how Madelaine Pierce and that mountain man Sangro did in fact find it and shared it fifty-fifty. Story has it that the woman finally left the mountains and used her wealth to spend her time livin' in luxury and travellin'; never in one place for long, never travellin' under the same name. But that's mebbe a story for the tellin' round the night fire on the trail. Who knows.'

'And that's it, folks,' smiled Merv Hinks glancing at the clock as he stepped from behind his counter. 'Here comes our fourth passenger, and right on time too.'

The woman drifted into the office from the board-walk with a hint of expensive perfume, a flashing smile and twinkling eyes. 'Good afternoon,' she murmured quietly.

'Afternoon, Miss Dixon,' smiled Merv. 'Stage is leavin' right on time, ma'am, and you're booked along of your fellow passengers clear through to

Rainwater. Matt Taylor's drivin' with Charlie Deakin here ridin' shotgun. Charlie's been with our line practically all his life. Knows the territory like the back of his hand.'

'I'm sure he does,' said Miss Dixon demurely, her gaze lingering on Charlie's face. 'Yes, I'm sure.'

'Shall we get loaded, ma'am?' bustled Merv, taking the woman's valise.

'By all means.'

'This your first trip across the desert, ma'am?' grinned the cattleman, eyeing the generous cut of the woman's plunging neckline.

'No, I've travelled this way before, but many years ago.' She glanced quickly at Charlie. 'But I've quite forgotten the experience.' She took the cattleman's arm and walked towards the open door. 'Tell me about yourself,' she cooed. 'You look to be a man of the world.'

'Hussy!' muttered the lady in the hat.

Merv waited until the passengers had climbed aboard before drawing Charlie aside. 'Know somethin',' he murmured, 'if I wasn't seein' it for myself I'd say that Miss Dixon is the spittin' image of Madelaine Pierce, her dead-eyed double.'

'No, I reckon not,' said Charlie thoughtfully, watching as the woman chatted amiably to her fellow passengers. 'You've been behind that counter of yours too long, Merv, seen too many faces. Mebbe we should call it a day. We've seen it all, ain't we? You bet.' He slapped Merv on the back. 'Let's get this outfit rollin', eh? One more trip for old-time's sake . . . '

## THE END

## THE JAYHAWKERS

### Elliot Conway

Luther Kane, one-time captain with Colonel Mosby's raiders, is forced to leave Texas; bounty hunters are tracking down and arresting men who served with the colonel during the Civil War. He joins up with three Missouri brush boys, outlawed by the Union government, and themselves hunted for atrocities committed whilst riding with 'Bloody' Bill Anderson. Now, in a series of bloody shoot-outs, they must take the fight to the red legs to finally end the war against them . . .

# VENGEANCE AT BITTERSWEET

## Dale Graham

Always a loner, Largo reckoned it was the reason for his survival as a bounty hunter. But things change when he has to join forces with Colonel Sebastian Kyte in the hunt for a band of desperate killers. Kyte is not interested in financial rewards. So what is the old Confederate soldier's game? And how does a Kiowa medicine man's daughter figure in the final showdown at Bittersweet? Vengeance is sweet, but it comes with a heavy price tag.

# DEVIL'S RANGE

## Skeeter Dodds

Caleb Ross had agreed to join his old friend Tom Watson as a ranching partner in Ghost Creek, and arrives full of optimism. But he rides into big trouble. Tom has been gunned down by Jack Sweeney of the Rawl range, mentor in mayhem to Scott Rawl . . . Enraged, Caleb heads for the ranch seeking vengeance for Tom's murder. But, up against a crooked law force and formidable opposition, he'll have to be quick and clever if he's to survive . . .

# THE COYOTE KIDS

## David Bingley

When Billy Bartram met Della Rhodes, he was led to contact her brother, Sandy East, one of the Coyote Kids. Billy's determined vendetta against Long John Carrick — a veteran renegade and gang leader — made him an ally of the Coyote Kids. Carrick's boys were hounding them to grab some valued treasure, but only the Kids knew of its location. When Red Murdo, the other Kid became a casualty, Sandy and Billy had to fight for their very existence . . . as well as for the treasure.